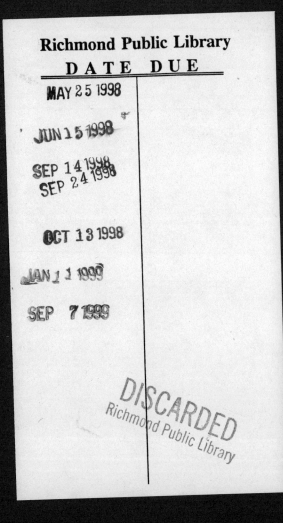

THE POSSIBILITY OF ANGELS

THE POSSIBILITY OF ANGELS

A Literary Anthology

Edited by Sophie Biriotti
Illustrations by Peter Malone

THE ARTWORKS PRESS, LONDON

CHRONICLE BOOKS
SAN FRANCISCO

Printed in Hong Kong
Designed by Michele Wetherbee
Pages 143–144 constitute a continuation of the
    copyright page.
The title *The Possibility of Angels* is taken from the poetry
    collection *The Possibility of Angels* by Keith Bosley
    (Macmillan, 1969).

Library of Congress Cataloging-in-Publication Data

The possibility of angels : a literary anthology / edited by
Sophie Biriotti ; illustrations by Peter Malone.
    144 p.   19 x 24.2 cm
    ISBN 0-8118-1530-7
    1. Angels—Literary collections. I. Biriotti, Sophie. II.
Malone, Peter, 1953–
    PN6071.A65P67   1997
    808.8'038291215—dc21   96-53498
                                            CIP

Distributed in Canada by
Raincoast Books
8680 Cambie Street
Vancouver, B.C. V6P 6M9

10 9 8 7 6 5 4 3 2 1

Chronicle Books
85 Second Street
San Francisco, CA 94105

Web site: www.chronbooks.com

To Michael and Amanda Doran. P.M.

Thanks to Christina Paouros for her invaluable
research assistance, and to Maurice, always. S.B.

TABLE OF CONTENTS

PREFACE

"What are angels made of?" "How many angels can fit on the head of a pin?" Medieval scholars and theologians worried about such questions for months on end. Small wonder—angels are the ultimate enigma: they are immortal, and yet their presence is always fleeting; magnificent in all their physical splendor, yet substanceless; divine, yet often human in appearance. As messengers from the world beyond, angels represent the dazzling possibility of absolute clarity, yet they remain unfathomable.

The conundrum that angels propose has fired the imagination of the greatest writers and thinkers around the world: What would it be like to talk to an angel? Can an angel be touched? How does one feel the presence of an angel? These questions are the stuff of legend and folklore, and the pieces collected in this volume represent the finest examples of the human imagination inspired by the concept of these mysterious and elusive creatures.

We think of angels as benign and untroubling, but let us not forget that the comfort they bring is not always easily attained: even in the most orthodox writings, an encounter with an angel can be difficult and painful. In the Book of Genesis, the patriarch Jacob wrestles with an angel and loses part of his thigh bone before he can be blessed and given the proud name. For all their mercy and their benevolent guardianship of humankind, angels can inflict a radical and uncomfortable shift in our perception of reality. Many of the stories in this collection tell of the strangeness and the intensity of an encounter with beings from another dimension: the violent irruption of the supernatural into the everyday, the spectacular into the mundane.

Other texts in this volume deal with the difficulty and struggle of recognition. In Bernard Malamud's *Angel Levine*, for instance, a simple and devout tailor refuses to recognize as an angel the strange black Jew who comes to save him. Only in the face of impending disaster does the tailor acknowledge his guardian, and through that struggle he acquires a greater wisdom in his devotion.

For many writers, the question is not only what we can learn about angels, but what they might have to learn from us. In Tolstoy's masterly tale *What Men Live By*, a fallen angel is sent to earth to learn how human beings live. He embarks on his quest by descending into the harshness and solitude of destitution. Given shelter by a shoemaker and his wife, he comes to learn the wonder of being mortal.

The encounter with an angel is a two-way process: the lessons exchanged between mortal and immortal are mutual. Nowhere is this more beautifully expressed than in Allan Gurganus's *It Had Wings*, a portrait of an angel crash-landing in an old woman's backyard. The angel must recover his strength to fly off again, and draws sustenance from the old woman's woes; she in turn feels her spirit lifted by his presence. The two become intertwined in an exquisite symbiosis.

The nature of our relationship with angels holds an enduring fascination. The texts in this collection come from a wide variety of places and times. There is also a huge variety of tones, from the passionate devotion of Blake's evocations to the absurdity of Kafka's disappointment, from Macrina Wiederkehr's exuberant celebration to Flannery O'Connor's hilarious tale of rebellion.

What all the pieces have in common is fine writing. It is scarcely surprising that angels have inspired so many dazzling displays of verbal creativity. Like angels, words—substanceless, ephemeral—communicate with a mysterious power. The Greeks used to speak of words having wings, and in the hands of the brilliant writers collected here, words can give flight to the imagination. Illuminating the text, Peter Malone's breathtaking illustrations offer a glimpse of what these texts allude to: the incomparable vision of wonder.

As you read this volume, listen carefully. Beneath the sound of the pages as you turn them, that faint, unfathomable sound is the rustling of wings as angels take flight.

Macrina Wiederkehr

FROM A TREE FULL OF ANGELS

Standing still for a moment, I see the first rays of sunlight shimmering through a silver maple tree. It is truly a moment of wonder, resplendent with light. I stand gazing as one in the midst of a vision. Suddenly I am uncertain whether those golden arms swaying in the morning sunlight are tree branches or angel wings. Such shining I find overpowering. My wondering heart is filled with joy.

And then in a twinkling I'm certain. I am standing before a tree full of angels dazzling me with their glorious presence. Bright wings of fire all aglow. Such beauty! Celestial bodies trembling in the trees! Trembling in awe over the beauty of a world that I take for granted. A tree bespangled with glory! Radiant Light! Angel wings, like stars, glistening in every branch. It's gold and silver everywhere I look.

So what do I do? What do I do with this vision that heaven has blessed me with? If I am an adult I keep very quiet about this vision, carefully guarding my reputation. I tell no one. If I am a child, or if I have a child's heart, I cannot contain the vision. I shout it from the rooftops. I say, "Listen, everybody! I saw a tree full of angels shining like stars in the night."

Can you not believe this? Come now, don't be a cynic. Your heart was made for deep things. Your entire being was designed for visions.

Robert Bridges

Spirits

12

Angel spirits of sleep,
White-robed, with silver hair,
In your meadows fair,
Where the willows weep,
And the sad moonbeam
On the gliding stream
Writes her scattered dream:

Angel spirits of sleep,
Dancing to the weir
In the hollow roar
Of its waters deep;
Know ye how men say
That ye haunt no more
Isle and grassy shore
With your moonlit play;
That ye dance not here;
White-robed spirits of sleep,
All the summer night
Threading dances light?

Gabriel García Márquez

A Very Old Man With

Enormous Wings A Tale For Children

On the third day of rain they had killed so many crabs inside the house that Pelayo had to cross his drenched courtyard and throw them into the sea, because the newborn child had a temperature all night and they thought it was due to the stench. The world had been sad since Tuesday. Sea and sky were a single ash-gray thing and the sands of the beach, which on March nights glimmered like powdered light, had become a stew of mud and rotten shellfish. The light was so weak at noon that when Pelayo was coming back to the house after throwing away the crabs, it was hard for him to see what it was that was moving and groaning in the rear of the courtyard. He had to go very close to see that it was an old man, a very old man, lying face down in the mud, who, in spite of his tremendous efforts, couldn't get up, impeded by his enormous wings.

Frightened by that nightmare, Pelayo ran to get Elisenda, his wife, who was putting compresses on the sick child, and he took her to the rear of the courtyard. They both looked at the fallen body with mute stupor. He was dressed like a rag-picker. There were only a few faded hairs left on his bald skull and very few teeth in his mouth, and his pitiful condition of a drenched great-grandfather had taken away any sense of grandeur he might have had. His huge buzzard wings, dirty and half-plucked, were forever entangled in the mud. They looked at him so long and so closely that Pelayo and Elisenda very soon overcame their surprise and in the end found him familiar. Then they dared speak to him, and he answered in an incomprehensible dialect with a strong sailor's voice. That was how they skipped over the inconvenience of the wings and quite intelligently concluded that he was a lonely castaway from some foreign ship wrecked by the storm. And yet, they called in a neighbor woman who knew everything about life and death to see him, and all she needed was one look to show them their mistake.

"He's an angel," she told them. "He must have been coming for the child, but the poor fellow is so old that the rain knocked him down."

On the following day everyone knew that a flesh-and-blood angel was held captive in Pelayo's house. Against the judgment of the wise neighbor woman, for whom angels in those times were the fugitive survivors of a celestial conspiracy, they did not have the heart to club him to death. Pelayo watched over him all afternoon from the kitchen, armed with his bailiff's club, and before going to bed he dragged him out of the mud and locked him up with the hens in the wire chicken coop. In the middle of the night, when the rain stopped, Pelayo and Elisenda were still killing crabs. A short time afterward the child woke up without a fever and with a desire to eat. Then they felt magnanimous and decided to put the angel on a raft with fresh water and provisions for three days and leave him to his fate on the high seas. But when they went out into the courtyard with the first light of dawn, they found the whole neighborhood in front of the chicken coop having fun with the angel, without the slightest reverence, tossing him things to eat through the openings in the wire as if he weren't a supernatural creature but a circus animal.

Father Gonzaga arrived before seven o'clock, alarmed at the strange news. By that time onlookers less frivolous than those at dawn had already arrived and they were making all kinds of conjectures concerning the captive's future. The simplest among them thought that he should be named mayor of the world. Others of sterner mind felt that he should be promoted to the rank of five-star general in order to win all wars. Some visionaries hoped that he could be put to stud in order to implant on earth a race of winged wise men who could take charge of the universe. But Father Gonzaga, before becoming a priest, had been a robust woodcutter. Standing by the wire, he reviewed his catechism in an instant and asked them to open the door so that he could take a close look at the pitiful man who looked more like a huge decrepit hen among the fascinated chickens. He was lying in a corner drying his open wings in the sunlight among the fruit peels and breakfast leftovers that the early risers had thrown him. Alien to the impertinences of the world, he only lifted

his antiquarian eyes and murmured something in his dialect when Father Gonzaga went into the chicken coop and said good morning to him in Latin. The parish priest had his first suspicion of an imposter when he saw that he did not understand the language of God or know how to greet His ministers. Then he noticed that seen close up he was much too human: he had an unbearable smell of the outdoors, the back side of his wings was strewn with parasites and his main feathers had been mistreated by terrestrial winds, and nothing about him measured up to the proud dignity of angels. Then he came out of the chicken coop and in a brief sermon warned the curious against the risks of being ingenuous. He reminded them that the devil had the bad habit of making use of carnival tricks in order to confuse the unwary. He argued that if wings were not the essential element in determining the difference between a hawk and an airplane, they were even less so in the recognition of angels. Nevertheless, he promised to write a letter to his bishop so that the latter would write to his primate so that the latter would write to the Supreme Pontiff in order to get the final verdict from the highest courts.

His prudence fell on sterile hearts. The news of the captive angel spread with such rapidity that after a few hours the courtyard had the bustle of a marketplace

and they had to call in troops with fixed bayonets to disperse the mob that was about to knock the house down. Elisenda, her spine all twisted from sweeping up so much marketplace trash, then got the idea of fencing in the yard and charging five cents admission to see the angel.

The curious came from far away. A traveling carnival arrived with a flying acrobat who buzzed over the crowd several times, but no one paid any attention to him because his wings were not those of an angel but, rather, those of a sidereal bat. The most unfortunate invalids on earth came in search of health: a poor woman who since childhood had been counting her heartbeats and had run out of numbers; a Portuguese man who couldn't sleep because the noise of the stars disturbed him; a sleepwalker who got up at night to undo the things he had done while awake; and many others with less serious ailments. In the midst of that shipwreck disorder that made the earth tremble, Pelayo and Elisenda were happy with fatigue, for in less than a week they had crammed their rooms with money and the line of pilgrims waiting their turn to enter still reached beyond the horizon.

The angel was the only one who took no part in his own act. He spent his time trying to get comfortable in his borrowed nest, befuddled by the hellish heat of the oil lamps and sacramental candles that had been placed along the wire. At first they tried to make him eat some mothballs, which, according to the wisdom of the wise neighbor woman, were the food prescribed for angels. But he turned them down, just as he turned down the papal lunches that the penitents brought him, and they never found out whether it was because he was an angel or because he was an old man that in the end he ate nothing but eggplant mush. His only supernatural virtue seemed to be patience. Especially during the first days, when the hens pecked at him, searching for the stellar parasites that proliferated in his wings, and the cripples pulled out feathers to touch their defective parts with, and even the most merciful threw stones at him, trying to get him to rise so they could see him standing. The only time they succeeded in arousing him was when they burned his side with an iron for branding steers, for he had been motionless for so many hours that they thought he was dead. He awoke with a start, ranting in his hermetic language and with tears in his eyes, and he flapped his wings a couple of times, which brought on a whirlwind of chicken dung and lunar dust and a gale of panic that did not seem to be of this world. Although many thought that his reaction had been one not of rage but of pain, from then on they were careful not to annoy him, because the majority understood that his passivity was not that of a hero taking his ease but that of a cataclysm in repose.

Father Gonzaga held back the crowd's frivolity with formulas of maidservant inspiration while awaiting the arrival of a final judgment on the nature of the captive. But the mail from Rome showed no sense of urgency. They spent their time finding out if the prisoner had a navel, if his dialect had any connection with Aramaic, how many times he could fit on the head of a pin, or whether he wasn't just a Norwegian with wings. Those meager letters might have come and gone until the end of time if a providential event had not put an end to the priest's tribulations.

It so happened that during those days, among so many other carnival attractions, there arrived in town the traveling show of the woman who had been changed into a spider for having disobeyed her parents. The admission to see her was not only less than the admission to see the angel, but people were permitted to ask her all manner of questions about her absurd state and to examine her up and down so that no one would ever doubt the truth of her horror. She was a frightful tarantula the size of a ram and with the head of a sad maiden. What was most heartrending, however, was not her outlandish shape but the sincere affliction with which she recounted the details of her misfortune. While still practically a child she had sneaked out of her parents' house to go to a dance, and while she was coming back through the woods after having danced all night without permission, a

Gabriel

García

Márquez

fearful thunderclap rent the sky in two and through the crack came the lightning bolt of brimstone that changed her into a spider. Her only nourishment came from the meatballs that charitable souls chose to toss into her mouth. A spectacle like that, full of so much human truth and with such a fearful lesson, was bound to defeat without even trying that of a haughty angel who scarcely deigned to look at mortals. Besides, the few miracles attributed to the angel showed a certain mental disorder, like the blind man who didn't recover his sight but grew three new teeth, or the paralytic who didn't get to walk but almost won the lottery, and the leper whose sores sprouted sunflowers. Those consolation miracles, which were more like mocking fun, had already ruined the angel's reputation when the woman who had been changed into a spider finally crushed him completely. That was how Father Gonzaga was cured forever of his insomnia and Pelayo's courtyard went back to being as empty as during the time it had rained for three days and crabs walked through the bedrooms.

The owners of the house had no reason to lament. With the money they saved they built a two-story mansion with balconies and gardens and high netting so that crabs wouldn't get in during the winter, and with iron bars on the windows so that angels wouldn't get in. Pelayo also set up a rabbit warren close to town and gave up his job as bailiff for good, and Elisenda bought some satin pumps with high heels and many dresses of iridescent silk, the kind worn on Sunday by the most desirable women in those times. The chicken coop was the only thing that didn't receive any attention. If they washed it down with creolin and burned tears of myrrh inside it every so often, it was not in homage to the angel but to drive away the dungheap stench that still hung everywhere like a ghost and was turning the new house into an old one. At first, when the child learned to walk, they were careful that he not get too close to the chicken coop. But then they began to lose their fears and got used to the smell, and before the child got his second teeth he'd gone inside the chicken coop to play, where the wires were falling apart. The angel was no less standoffish with him than with other mortals, but he tolerated the most ingenious infamies with the patience of a dog who had no illusions. They both came down with chicken pox at the same time. The doctor who took care of the child couldn't resist the temptation to listen to the angel's heart, and he found so much whistling in the heart and so many sounds in his kidneys that it seemed impossible for him to be alive. What surprised him most, however, was the logic of his wings. They seemed so natural on that completely human organism that he couldn't understand why other men didn't have them too.

When the child began school it had been some time since the sun and rain had caused the collapse of the chicken coop. The angel went dragging himself about here and there like a stray dying man. They would drive him out of the bedroom with a broom and a moment later find him in the kitchen. He seemed to be in so many places at the same time that they grew to think that he'd been duplicated, that he was reproducing himself all through the house, and the exasperated and unhinged Elisenda shouted that it was awful living in that hell full of angels. He

could scarcely eat and his antiquarian eyes had also become so foggy that he went about bumping into posts. All he had left were the bare cannulae of his last feathers. Pelayo threw a blanket over him and extended him the charity of letting him sleep in the shed, and only then did they notice that he had a temperature at night, and was delirious with the tongue twisters of an old Norwegian. That was one of the few times they became alarmed, for they thought he was going to die and not even the wise neighbor woman had been able to tell them what to do with dead angels.

And yet he not only survived his worst winter, but seemed improved with the first sunny days. He remained motionless for several days in the farthest corner of the courtyard, where no one would see him, and at the beginning of December some large, stiff feathers began to grow on his wings, the feathers of a scarecrow, which looked more like another misfortune of decrepitude. But he must have known the reason for those changes, for he was quite careful that no one should notice them, that no one should hear the sea chanteys that he sometimes sang under the stars. One morning Elisenda was cutting some bunches of onions for lunch when a wind that seemed to come from the high seas blew into the kitchen. Then she went to the window and caught the angel in his first attempts at flight. They were so clumsy that his fingernails opened a furrow in the vegetable patch and he was on the point of knocking the shed down with the ungainly flapping that slipped on the light and couldn't get a grip on the air. But he did manage to gain altitude. Elisenda let out a sigh of relief, for herself and for him, when she saw him pass over the last houses, holding himself up in some way with the risky flapping of a senile vulture. She kept watching him even when she was through cutting the onions and she kept on watching until it was no longer possible for her to see him, because then he was no longer an annoyance in her life but an imaginary dot on the horizon of the sea.

22

G a b r i e l

G a r c í a

M á r q u e z

Do the Irish among you
recall the old poet
who loved Derry
for its crowd of white angels
from one end to another?

My townspeople (for so
this once I will address you)
consider
the possibility of angels

Keith   Bosley

THE POSSIBILITY OF ANGELS

not the transparencies
which holy men project
on to white minds
in dim chapels

but the kind we are told
we should not believe in
shutting our eyes
and hearts to them

who are demonstrated
not by the deduction
of man from god

but by their walking
past a butcher's shop
with white silk billowing
about their poised bodies.

Louis Ginzberg

FROM JACOB WRESTLES

WITH THE ANGEL

The servants of Jacob went before him with the present for Esau, and he followed with his wives and his children. As he was about to pass over the ford of Jabbok, he observed a shepherd, who likewise had sheep and camels. The stranger approached Jacob and proposed that they should ford the stream together, and help each other move their cattle over, and Jacob assented, on the condition that his possessions should be put across first. In the twinkling of an eye Jacob's sheep were transferred to the other side of the stream by the shepherd. Then the flocks of the shepherd were to be moved by Jacob, but no matter how many he took over to the opposite bank, always there remained some on the hither shore. There was no end to the cattle, though Jacob labored all the night through. At last he lost patience, and he fell upon the shepherd and caught him by the throat, crying out, "O thou wizard, thou wizard, at night no enchantment succeeds!" The angel thought, "Very well, let him know once and for all with whom he has had dealings," and with his finger he touched the earth, whence fire burst forth. But Jacob said, "What! Thou thinkest thus to affright me, who am made wholly of fire?"

The shepherd was no less a personage than the archangel Michael, and in his combat with Jacob he was assisted by the whole host of angels under his command. He was on the point of inflicting a dangerous wound upon Jacob, when God appeared, and all the angels, even Michael himself, felt their strength ooze away.

Seeing that he could not prevail against Jacob, the archangel touched the hollow of his thigh, and injured him, and God rebuked him, saying, "Dost thou act as is seemly, when thou causest a blemish in My priest Jacob?" Michael said in astonishment, "Why, it is I who am Thy priest!" But God said, "Thou art My priest in heaven, and he is My priest on earth." Thereupon Michael summoned the archangel Raphael, saying, "My comrade, I pray thee, help me out of my distress, for thou art charged with the healing of all disease," and Raphael cured Jacob of the injury Michael had inflicted.

The Lord continued to reproach Michael, saying, "Why didst thou do harm unto My first-born son?" and the archangel answered, "I did it only to glorify Thee," and then God appointed Michael as the guardian angel of Jacob and his seed unto the end of all generations, with these words:

"Thou art a fire, and so is Jacob a fire; thou art the head of the angels, and he is head of the nations; thou art supreme over all the angels, and he is supreme over all the peoples. Therefore he who is supreme over all the angels shall be appointed unto him who is supreme over all the peoples, that he may entreat mercy for him from the Supreme One over all."

Then Michael said unto Jacob, "How is it possible that thou who couldst prevail against me, the most distinguished of the angels, art afraid of Esau?"

When the day broke, Michael said to Jacob, "Let me go, for the day breaketh," but Jacob held him back, saying, "Art thou a thief, or a gambler with dice, that thou fearest the daylight?" At that moment appeared many different hosts of angels, and they called unto Michael: "Ascend, O Michael, the time of song hath come, and if thou art not in heaven to lead the choir, none will sing." And Michael entreated Jacob with supplications to let him go, for he feared the angels of Arabot would consume him with fire, if he were not there to start the songs of praise at the proper time. Jacob said, "I will not let thee go, except thou bless me," whereto Michael made reply: "Who is greater, the servant or the son? I am the servant, and thou art the son. Why, then, cravest thou my blessing?" Jacob urged as an argument, "The angels that visited Abraham did not leave without blessing him," but Michael held, "They were sent by God for that very purpose, and I was not." Yet Jacob insisted upon his demand, and Michael pleaded with him, saying, "The angels that betrayed a heavenly secret were banished from their place for one hundred and thirty-eight years. Dost thou desire that I should acquaint thee with what would cause my banishment likewise?" In the end the angel nevertheless had to yield; Jacob could not be moved, and Michael took counsel with himself thus: "I will reveal a secret to him, and if God demands to know why I revealed it, I will make answer, Thy children stand upon their wishes with Thee, and Thou dost yield to them. How, then, could I have left Jacob's wish unfulfilled?"

Louis

Ginzberg

Wallace Stevens

Angel Surrounded by Paysans

One of the countrymen:
There is
A welcome at the door to which no one comes?

The Angel:
I am the angel of reality,
Seen for a moment standing in the door.

I have neither ashen wing nor wear of ore
And live without a tepid aureole,

Or stars that follow me, not to attend,
But, of my being and its knowing, part.

I am one of you and being one of you
Is being and knowing what I am and know.

Yet I am the necessary angel of earth,
Since, in my sight, you see the earth again,

Cleared of its stiff and stubborn, man-locked set,
And, in my hearing, you hear its tragic drone

Rise liquidly in liquid lingerings,
Like watery words awash; like meanings said

By repetitions of half-meanings. Am I not,
Myself, only half of a figure of a sort,

A figure half seen, or seen for a moment, a man
Of the mind, an apparition apparelled in

Apparels of such lightest look that a turn
Of my shoulder and quickly, too quickly, I am gone?

32

Wallace

Stevens

John   Updike

Archangel

Onyx and split cedar and bronze vessels lowered into still water: these things I offer. Porphyry, teakwood, jasmine, and myrrh: these gifts I bring. The sheen of my sandals is dulled by the dust of cloves. My wings are waxed with nectar. My eyes are diamonds in whose facets red gold is mirrored. My face is a mask of ivory: Love me. Listen to my promises:

Cold water will drip from the intricately chased designs of the bronze vessels. Thick-lipped urns will sweat in the fragrant cellars. The orchards never weary of bearing on my islands. The very leaves give nourishment. The banked branches never crowd the paths. The grape vines will grow unattended. The very seeds of the berries are sweet nuts. Why do you smile? Have you never been hungry?

The workmanship of the bowers will be immaculate. Where the elements are joined, the sword of the thinnest whisper will find its point excluded. Where the beams have been tapered, each swipe of the plane is continuous. Where the wood needed locking, pegs of a counter grain have been driven. The ceilings are high, for coolness, and the spaced shingles seal at the first breath of mist. Though the windows are open, the eaves of the roof are so wide that nothing of the rain comes into the rooms but its scent. Mats of perfect cleanness cover the floor. The fire is cupped in black rock and sustained on a smooth breast of ash. Have you never lacked shelter?

Where, then, has your life been touched? My pleasures are as specific as they are everlasting. The sliced edges of a fresh ream of laid paper, cream, stiff, rag-rich. The freckles of the closed eyelids of a woman attentive in the first white blush of morning. The ball diminishing well down the broad green throat of the first at Cape Ann. The good catch, a candy sun slatting the bleachers. The fair at the vanished poorhouse. The white arms of girls dancing, taffeta, white arms violet in the hollows music its ecstasies praise the white wrists of praise the white arms and the white paper trimmed the Euclidean proof of Pythagoras' theorem its tightening beauty the iridescence of an old copper found in the salt sand. The microscopic glitter in the ink of the letters of words that are your own. Certain moments, remembered or imagined, of childhood. Three-handed pinochle by the brown glow of the stained-glass lampshade, your parents out of their godliness silently wishing you to win. The Brancusi room, silent. *Pines and Rocks*, by Cézanne; and *The Lace-Maker* in the Louvre hardly bigger than your spread hand.

Such glimmers I shall widen to rivers; nothing will be lost, not the least grain of remembered dust, and the multiplication shall be a thousand thousand fold; love me. Embrace me; come, touch my side, where honey flows. Do not be afraid. Why should my promises be vain? Jade and cinnamon: do you deny that such things exist? Why do you turn away? Is not my song a stream of balm? My arms are heaped with apples and ancient books; there is no harm in me; no. Stay. Praise me. Your praise of me is praise of yourself; wait. Listen. I will begin again.

Franz   Kafka

FROM 25TH JUNE, DIARIES 1914

25th June. I paced up and down my room from early morning until twilight. The window was open, it was a warm day. The noises of the narrow street beat in uninterruptedly. By now I knew every trifle in the room from having looked at it in the course of my pacing up and down. My eyes had travelled over every wall. I had pursued the pattern of the rug to its last convolution, noted every mark of age it bore. My fingers had spanned the table across the middle many times. I had already bared my teeth repeatedly at the picture of the landlady's dead husband.

Towards evening I walked over to the window and sat down on the low sill. Then, for the first time not moving restlessly about, I happened calmly to glance into the interior of the room and at the ceiling. And finally, finally, unless I were mistaken, this room which I had so violently upset began to stir. The tremor began at the edges of the thinly plastered white ceiling. Little pieces of plaster broke off and with a distinct thud fell here and there, as if at random, to the floor. I held out my hand and some plaster fell into it too; in my excitement I threw it over my head into the street without troubling to turn around. The cracks in the ceiling made no pattern yet, but it was already possible somehow to imagine one. But I put these games aside when a bluish violet began to mix with the white; it spread straight out from the centre of the ceiling, which itself remained white, even radiantly white, where the shabby electric lamp was stuck. Wave after wave of the colour—or was it a light?—spread out towards the now darkening edges. One no longer paid any attention to the plaster that was falling away as if under the pressure of a skilfully applied tool. Yellow and golden-yellow colours now penetrated the violet from the side. But the ceiling did not really take on these different hues; the colours merely made it somewhat transparent; things striving to break through seemed to be hovering above it, already one could almost see the outlines of a movement there, an arm was thrust out, a silver sword swung to and fro. It was meant for me, there was no doubt of that; a vision intended for my liberation was being prepared.

I sprang up on the table to make everything ready, tore out the electric light together with its brass fixture and hurled it to the floor, then jumped down and pushed the table from the middle of the room to the wall. That which was striving to appear could drop down unhindered on the carpet and announce to me whatever it had to announce. I had barely finished when the ceiling did in fact break open. In the dim light, still at a great height, I had judged it badly, an angel in bluish-violet robes girt with gold cords sank slowly down on great white silken-shining wings, the sword in its raised arm thrust out horizontally. "An angel, then!" I thought; "it has been flying towards me all the day and in my disbelief I did not know it. Now it will speak to me." I lowered my eyes. When I raised them again the angel was still there, it is true, hanging rather far off under the ceiling (which had closed again), but it was no living angel, only a painted wooden figurehead off the prow of some ship, one of the kind that hangs from the ceiling in sailors' taverns, nothing more.

The hilt of the sword was made in such a way as to hold candles and catch the dripping tallow. I had pulled the electric light down; I didn't want to remain in the dark, there was still one candle left, so I got up on a chair, stuck the candle into the hilt of the sword, lit it, and then sat late into the night under the angel's faint flame.

J o h n   R o n n e r

Saints and their Angels

St. Frances of Rome (1384–1440) allegedly received a "light blow heard by all" from her guardian angel when he was displeased with her.

St. Francisca, who lived in the 1400s, had a guardian angel whose face was so brilliantly white, she could read her midnight prayers by its glow.

Bernard   Malamud

Angel Levine

Manischevitz, a tailor, in his fifty-first year suffered many reverses and indignities. Previously a man of comfortable means, he overnight lost all he had, when his establishment caught fire and, after a metal container of cleaning fluid exploded, burned to the ground. Although Manischevitz was insured against fire, damage suits by two customers who had been hurt in the flames deprived him of every penny he had collected. At almost the same time, his son, of much promise, was killed in the war, and his daughter, without so much as a word of warning, married a lout and disappeared with him as off the face of the earth. Thereafter Manischevitz was victimized by excruciating backaches and found himself unable to work even as a presser—the only kind of work available to him—for more than an hour or two daily, because beyond that the pain from standing became maddening. His Fanny, a good wife and mother, who had taken in washing and sewing, began before his eyes to waste away. Suffering shortness of breath, she at last became seriously ill and took to her bed. The doctor, a former customer of Manischevitz, who out of pity treated them, at first had difficulty diagnosing her ailment but later put it down as hardening of the arteries at an advanced stage. He took Manischevitz aside, prescribed complete rest for her, and in whispers gave him to know there was little hope.

Throughout his trials Manischevitz had remained somewhat stoic, almost unbelieving that all this had descended upon his head, as if it were happening, let us say, to an acquaintance or some distant relative; it was in sheer quantity of woe incomprehensible. It was also ridiculous, unjust, and because he had always been a religious man, it was in a way an affront to God. Manischevitz believed this in all his suffering. When his burden had grown too crushingly heavy to be borne he prayed in his chair with shut hollow eyes: "My Dear God, sweetheart, did I deserve that this should happen to me?" Then recognizing the worthlessness of it, he put aside the complaint and prayed humbly for assistance: "Give Fanny back her health, and to me for myself that I shouldn't feel pain in every step. Help now or tomorrow is too late. This I don't have to tell you." And Manischevitz wept.

Manischevitz's flat, which he had moved into after the disastrous fire, was a meager one, furnished with a few sticks of chairs, a table, and bed, in one of the poorer sections of the city. There were three rooms: a small, poorly-papered living room; an apology for a kitchen, with a wooden icebox; and the comparatively large bedroom where Fanny lay in a sagging secondhand bed, gasping for breath. The bedroom was the warmest room of the house and it was here, after his outburst to God, that Manischevitz, by the light of two small bulbs overhead, sat reading his Jewish newspaper. He was not truly reading, because his thoughts were everywhere; however the print offered a convenient resting place for his eyes, and a word or two, when he permitted himself to comprehend them, had the momentary effect of helping him forget his troubles. After a short while he discovered, to his surprise, that he was actively scanning the news, searching for an item of great interest to him. Exactly what he thought he would read he couldn't say—until he realized, with some astonishment, that he was expecting to discover something about himself. Manischevitz put his paper down and looked up with the distinct impression that someone had entered the apartment, though he could not remember having heard the sound of the door opening. He looked around: the room was very still, Fanny sleeping, for once, quietly. Half-frightened, he watched her until he was satisfied she wasn't dead; then, still disturbed by the thought of an unannounced visitor, he stumbled into the living room and there had the shock of his life, for at the table sat a Negro reading a newspaper he had folded up to fit into one hand.

"What do you want here?" Manischevitz asked in fright.

The Negro put down the paper and glanced up with a gentle expression. "Good evening." He seemed not to be sure of himself, as if he had got into the wrong house. He was a large man, bonily built, with a heavy head covered by a hard derby, which he made no attempt to remove. His eyes seemed sad, but his lips, above which he wore a slight mustache, sought to smile; he was not otherwise prepossessing. The cuffs of his sleeves, Manischevitz noted, were frayed to the lining and the dark suit was badly fitted. He had very large feet. Recovering from his fright, Manischevitz guessed he had left the door open and was being visited by a case worker from the Welfare Department—some came at night—for he had recently applied for relief. Therefore he lowered himself into a chair opposite the Negro, trying, before the man's uncertain smile, to feel comfortable. The former tailor sat stiffly but patiently at the table, waiting for the investigator to take out his pad and pencil and begin asking questions; but before long he became convinced the man intended to do nothing of the sort.

"Who are you?" Manischevitz at last asked uneasily.

"If I may, insofar as one is able to, identify myself, I bear the name of Alexander Levine."

In spite of all his troubles Manischevitz felt a smile growing on his lips. "You said Levine?" he politely inquired.

The Negro nodded. "That is exactly right."

Carrying the jest farther, Manischevitz asked, "You are maybe Jewish?"

"All my life I was, willingly."

The tailor hesitated. He had heard of black Jews but had never met one. It gave an unusual sensation.

Recognizing in afterthought something odd about the tense of Levine's remark, he said doubtfully, "You ain't Jewish anymore?"

Levine at this point removed his hat, revealing a very white part in his black hair, but quickly replaced it. He replied, "I have recently been disincarnated into an angel. As such, I offer you my humble assistance, if to offer is within my province and ability—in the best sense." He lowered his eyes in apology. "Which calls for added explanation: I am what I am granted to be, and at present the completion is in the future."

"What kind of angel is this?" Manischevitz gravely asked.

"A bona fide angel of God, within prescribed limitations," answered Levine, "not to be confused with the members of any particular sect, order, or organization here on earth operating under a similar name."

Manischevitz was thoroughly disturbed. He had been expecting something but

43

Bernard

Malamud

not this. What sort of mockery was it—provided Levine was an angel—of a faithful servant who had from childhood lived in the synagogues, always concerned with the word of God?

To test Levine he asked, "Then where are your wings?"

The Negro blushed as well as he was able. Manischevitz understood this from his changed expression. "Under certain circumstances we lose privileges and prerogatives upon returning to earth, no matter for what purpose, or endeavoring to assist whosoever."

"So tell me," Manischevitz said triumphantly, "how did you get here?"

"I was transmitted."

Still troubled, the tailor said, "If you are a Jew, say the blessing for bread."

Levine recited it in sonorous Hebrew.

Although moved by the familiar words Manischevitz still felt doubt that he was dealing with an angel.

"If you are an angel," he demanded somewhat angrily, "give me the proof."

Levine wet his lips. "Frankly, I cannot perform either miracles or near miracles, due to the fact that I am in a condition of probation. How long that will persist or even consist, I admit, depends on the outcome."

Manischevitz racked his brains for some means of causing Levine positively to reveal his true identity, when the Negro spoke again:

"It was given me to understand that both your wife and you require assistance of a salubrious nature?"

The tailor could not rid himself of the feeling that he was the butt of a jokester. Is this what a Jewish angel looks like? he asked himself. This I am not convinced.

He asked a last question. "So if God sends to me an angel, why a black? Why not a white that there are so many of them?"

"It was my turn to go next," Levine explained.

Manischevitz could not persuaded. "I think you are a faker."

Levine slowly rose. His eyes showed disappointment and worry. "Mr. Manischevitz," he said tonelessly, "if you should desire me to be of assistance to you any time in the near future, or possibly before, I can be found"—he glanced at his fingernails—"in Harlem."

He was by then gone.

The next day Manischevitz felt some relief from his backache and was able to work four hours at pressing. The day after, he put in six hours; and the third day four again. Fanny sat up a little and asked for some halvah to suck. But on the fourth day the stabbing, breaking ache afflicted his back, and Fanny again lay supine, breathing with blue-lipped difficulty.

Manischevitz was profoundly disappointed at the return of his active pain and suffering. He had hoped for a longer interval of easement, long enough to have some thought other than of himself and his troubles. Day by day, hour by hour, minute after minute, he lived in pain, pain his only memory, questioning the necessity of it, inveighing against it, also, though with affection, against God. Why so *much*, Gottenyu? If He wanted to teach His servant a lesson for some reason, some cause—the nature of His nature—to teach him, say, for reasons of his weakness, his pride, perhaps, during his years of prosperity, his frequent neglect of God—to give him a little lesson, why then any of the tragedies that had happened to him, any *one* would have sufficed to chasten him. But *all together*—the loss of both his children, his means of livelihood, Fanny's health and his—that was too much to ask one frail-boned man to endure. Who, after all, was Manischevitz that he had been given so much to suffer? A tailor. Certainly not a man of talent. Upon him suffering was largely wasted. It went nowhere, into nothing: into more suffering. His pain did not earn him bread, nor fill the cracks in the wall, nor lift, in the middle of the night, the kitchen table; only lay upon him, sleepless, so sharply oppressively that he could many times have cried out yet not heard himself through this thickness of misery.

In this mood he gave no thought to Mr. Alexander Levine, but at moments when the pain waivered, slightly diminishing, he sometimes wondered if he had been mistaken to dismiss him. A black Jew and angel to boot—very hard to believe, but suppose he had been sent to succor him, and he, Manischevitz, was in his blindness too blind to comprehend? It was this thought that put him on the knife-point of agony.

Therefore the tailor, after much self-questioning and continuing doubt, decided he would seek the self-styled angel in Harlem. Of course he had great difficulty, because he had not asked for specific directions, and movement was tedious to him. The subway took him to 116th Street, and from there he wandered in the dark world. It was vast and its lights lit nothing. Everywhere were shadows, often moving. Manischevitz hobbled along with the aid of a cane, and not knowing where to seek in the blackened tenement buildings, look fruitlessly through store windows. In the stores he saw people and *everybody* was black. It was an amazing thing to observe. When he was too tired, too unhappy to go farther, Manischevitz stopped in front of a tailor's store. Out of familiarity with the appearance of it, with some sadness he entered. The tailor, an old skinny Negro with a mop of woolly gray hair, was sitting cross-legged on his workbench, sewing a pair of full-dress pants that had a razor slit all the way down the seat.

"You'll excuse me, please, gentleman," said Manischevitz, admiring the tailor's deft, thimbled fingerwork, "but you know maybe somebody by the name Alexander Levine?"

The tailor, who Manischevitz thought, seemed a little antagonistic to him, scratched his scalp.

"Cain't say I ever heared dat name."

"Alex-ander Lev-ine," Manischevitz repeated it.

The man shook his head. "Cain't say I heared."

About to depart, Manischevitz remembered to say: "He is an angel, maybe."

"Oh *him*," said the tailor clucking. "He hang out in dat honky tonk down here a ways." He pointed with his skinny finger and returned to the pants.

Manischevitz crossed the street against a red light and was almost run down by a taxi. On the block after the next, the sixth store from the corner was a cabaret, and the name in sparkling lights was Bella's. Ashamed to go in, Manischevitz gazed through the neon-lit window, and when the dancing couples had parted and drifted away he discovered at a table on the side, towards the rear, Levine.

He was sitting alone, a cigarette butt hanging from the corner of his mouth, playing solitaire with a dirty pack of cards, and Manischevitz felt a touch of pity for him, for Levine had deteriorated in appearance. His derby was dented and had a gray smudge on the side. His ill-fitting suit was shabbier, as if he had been sleeping in it. His shoes and trouser cuffs were muddy, and his face was covered with an impenetrable stubble the color of licorice. Manischevitz, though deeply disappointed, was about to enter, when a big-breasted Negress in a purple evening gown appeared before Levine's table, and with much laughter through many white teeth, broke into a vigorous shimmy. Levine looked straight at Manischevitz with a haunted expression, but the tailor was too paralyzed to move or acknowledge it. As Bella's gyrations continued, Levine rose, his eyes lit in excitement. She embraced him with vigor, both his hands clasped around her big restless buttocks and they tangoed together across the floor, loudly applauded by the noisy customers. She seemed to have lifted Levine off his feet and his large shoes hung limp as they danced. They slid past the windows where Manischevitz, white-faced, stood staring in. Levine winked slyly and the tailor left for home.

Fanny lay at death's door. Through shrunken lips she muttered concerning her childhood, the sorrows of the marriage bed, the loss of her children, yet wept to live. Manischevitz tried not to listen, but even without ears he would have heard. It was not a gift. The doctor panted up the stairs, a broad but bland, unshaven man (it was Sunday) and soon shook his head. A day at most, or two. He left at once, not without pity, to spare himself Manischevitz's multiplied sorrow; the man who never stopped hurting. He would someday get him into a public home.

Manischevitz visited a synagogue and there spoke to God, but God had absented himself. The tailor searched his heart and found no hope. When she died he would live dead. He considered taking his life although he knew he wouldn't. Yet it was something to consider. Considering, you existed. He railed against God— Can you love a rock, a broom, an emptiness? Baring his chest, he smote the naked bones, cursing himself for having believed.

Asleep in a chair that afternoon, he dreamed of Levine. He was standing before

Bernard

Malamud

a faded mirror, preening small decaying opalescent wings. "This means," mumbled Manischevitz, as he broke out of sleep, "that it is possible he could be an angel." Begging a neighbor lady to look in on Fanny and occasionally wet her lips with a few drops of water, he drew on his thin coat, gripped his walking stick, exchanged some pennies for a subway token, and rode to Harlem. He knew this act was the last desperate one of his woe: to go without belief, seeking a black magician to restore his wife to invalidism. Yet if there was no choice, he did at least what was chosen.

He hobbled to Bella's but the place had changed hands. It was now, as he breathed, a synagogue in a store. In the front, towards him, were several rows of empty wooden benches. In the rear stood the Ark, its portals of rough wood covered with rainbows of sequins; under it a long table on which lay the sacred scroll unrolled, illuminated by the dim light from a bulb on a chain overhead. Around the table, as if frozen to it and the scroll, which they all touched with their fingers, sat four Negroes wearing skullcaps. Now as they read the Holy Word, Manischevitz could, through the plate glass window, hear the singsong chant of their voices. One of them was old with a gray beard. One was bubble-eyed. One was hump-backed. The fourth was a boy, no older than thirteen. Their heads moved in rhythmic swaying. Touched by this sight from his childhood and youth, Manischevitz entered and stood silent in the rear.

"Neshoma," said bubble eyes, pointing to the word with a stubby finger. "Now what dat mean?"

"That's the word that means soul," said the boy. He wore glasses.

"Let's git on wid de commentary," said the old man.

"Ain't necessary," said the humpback. "Souls is immaterial substance. That's all. The soul is derived in that manner. The immateriality is derived from the substance, and they both, causally an' otherwise, derived from the soul. There can be no higher."

"That's the highest."

"Over de top."

"Wait a minute," said bubble eyes. "I don't see what is dat immaterial substance. How come de one gits hitched up to de odder?" He addressed the humpback.

"Ask me something hard. Because it is substanceless immateriality. It couldn't be closer together, like all the parts of the body under one skin—closer."

"Hear now," said the old man.

"All you done is switched de words."

"It's the primum mobile, the substanceless substance from which comes all things that were incepted in the idea—you, me and everything and body else."

"Now how did all dat happen? Make it sound simple."

"It de speerit," said the old man. "On de face of de water moved de speerit. An' dat was good. It say so in de Book. From de speerit ariz de man."

"But now listen here. How come it become substance if it all de time a spirit?"

"God alone done dat."

"Holy! Holy! Praise His Name."

"But has dis spirit got some kind of a shade or color?" asked bubble eyes, deadpan.

"Man of course not. A spirit is a spirit."

"Then how come we is colored?" he said with a triumphant glare.

"Ain't got nothing to do wid dat."

"I still like to know."

"God put the spirit in all things," answered the boy. "He put it in the green leaves and the yellow flowers. He put it with the gold in the fishes and the blue in the sky. That's how come it came to us."

"Amen."

"Praise Lawd and utter loud His speechless name."

"Blow de bugle till it bust the sky."

They fell silent, intent upon the next word. Manischevitz approached them.

"You'll excuse me," he said. "I am looking for Alexander Levine. You know him maybe?"

"That's the angel," said the boy.

"Oh, *him*," snuffed bubble eyes.

"You'll find him at Bella's. It's the establishment right across the street," the humpback said.

Manischevitz said he was sorry that he could not stay, thanked them, and limped across the street. It was already night. The city was dark and he could barely find his way.

But Bella's was bursting with the blues. Through the window Manischevitz recognized the dancing crowd and among them sought Levine. He was sitting loose-lipped at Bella's side table. They were tippling from an almost empty whiskey fifth. Levine had shed his old clothes, wore a shiny new checkered suit, pearl-gray derby,

cigar, and big, two-tone button shoes. To the tailor's dismay, a drunken look had settled upon his formerly dignified face. He leaned towards Bella, tickled her ear lobe with his pinky, while whispering words that sent her into gales of raucous laughter. She fondled his knee.

Manischevitz, girding himself, pushed open the door and was not welcomed.

"This place reserved."

"Beat it, pale puss."

"Exit, Yankel, Semitic trash."

But he moved towards the table where Levine sat, the crowd breaking before him as he hobbled forward.

"Mr. Levine," he spoke in a trembly voice. "Is here Manischevitz."

Levine glared blearily. "Speak yo' piece, son."

Manischevitz shuddered. His back plagued him. Cold tremors tormented his crooked legs. He looked around, everybody was all ears.

"You'll excuse me. I would like to talk to you in a private place."

"Speak, Ah is a private pusson."

Bella laughed piercingly. "Stop it, boy, you killin' me."

Manischevitz, no end disturbed, considered fleeing but Levine addressed him:

"Kindly state the pu'pose of yo' communication with yo's truly."

The tailor wet cracked lips. "You are Jewish. This I am sure."

Levine rose, nostrils flaring. "Anythin' else yo' got to say?"

Manischevitz's tongue lay like stone.

"Speak now or fo'ever hold off."

Tears blinded the tailor's eyes. Was ever man so tried? Should he say he believed a half-drunken Negro to be an angel?

The silence slowly petrified.

Manischevitz was recalling scenes of his youth as a wheel in his mind whirred: believe, do not, yes, no, yes, no. The pointer pointed to yes, to between yes and no, to no, no it was yes. He sighed. It moved but one had still to make a choice.

"I think you are an angel from God." He said it in a broken voice, thinking, If you said it it was said. If you believed it you must say it. If you believed, you believed.

The hush broke. Everybody talked but the music began and they went on dancing. Bella, grown bored, picked up the cards and dealt herself a hand.

Levine burst into tears. "How you have humiliated me."

Manischevitz apologized.

"Wait'll I freshen up." Levine went to the men's room and returned in his old clothes.

No one said goodbye as they left.

They rode to the flat via subway. As they walked up the stairs Manischevitz pointed with his cane at his door.

"That's all been taken care of," Levine said. "You best go in while I take off."

Disappointed that it was so soon over but torn by curiosity, Manischevitz followed the angel up three flights to the roof. When he got there the door was already padlocked.

Luckily he could see through a small broken window. He heard an odd noise, as though of a whirring of wings, and when he strained for a wider view, could have sworn he saw a dark figure borne aloft on a pair of magnificent black wings.

A feather drifted down. Manischevitz gasped as it turned white, but it was only snowing.

He rushed downstairs. In the flat Fanny wielded a dust mop under the bed and then upon the cobwebs on the wall.

"A wonderful thing, Fanny," Manischevitz said. "Believe me, there are Jews everywhere."

Allan Cunningham

William Blake Talks
about Angels

According to Allan Cunningham, Blake's companion for nine years:

Blake claimed to see angels in trees on his long London walks. He also believed that angels descended to the painters of old, and sat for their portraits.

When he sat to Phillips for the portrait engraved by Schiavonetti, the artist tried some small talk to make Blake relaxed and natural. He dared to question Michelangelo's ability to paint angels. "He could not paint an angel so well as Raphael."

Blake replied that Michelangelo painted *better* than Raphael: "I never *saw* any of the paintings of Michelangelo, but I speak from the opinion of a friend who could not be mistaken."

"A valuable friend, truly, and who may he be?"

"The archangel Gabriel, Sir."

"Was it not an evil spirit assuming a guise?"

"No. I was one day reading Young's *Night Thoughts*, and when I came to that passage which asks 'who can paint an angel?' I closed the book and cried, 'Aye! *Who* can paint an angel?' A voice in the room answered 'Michelangelo could.' 'And how do you know?' I said, looking around me, but saw nothing save a greater light than usual. 'I *know*,' said the voice, 'for I sat to him: I am the archangel Gabriel.' 'Oho!' I answered, 'You are, are you? I must have better assurance than *that* of a wandering voice; you may be an evil spirit—there are such in the land.' 'You shall have good assurance,' said the voice. 'Can an evil spirit do *this*? . . .'"

"And I looked whence the voice came, and was then aware of a shining shape, with bright wings, who diffused much light. As I looked, the shape dilated more and more: he waved his hands; the roof of my study opened; he ascended into heaven; stood in the Sun, and beckoning to me, moved the Universe. An angel of evil could not have done that—it was the archangel Gabriel."

Phillips marvelled much at this wild story; but caught from Blake's looks, as he related it, that rapt poetic expression which has rendered his portrait one of the finest of the English school.

54

A l l a n

C u n n i n g h a m

William Blake

The Angel

I dreamt a dream! What can it mean?
And that I was a maiden Queen
Guarded by an Angel mild:
Witless woe was ne'er beguiled!

And I wept both night and day,
And he wiped my tears away;
And I wept both day and night,
And hid from him my heart's delight.

So he took his wings and fled;
Then the morn blushed rosy red.
I dried my tears and armed my fears
With ten thousand shields and spears.

Soon my Angel came again;
I was armed, he came in vain;
For the time of youth was fled,
And grey hairs were on my head.

Emily Dickinson

Angels, in the
Early Morning

Angels, in the early morning   59
May be seen the Dews among,
Stooping—plucking—smiling—flying—
Do the Buds to them belong?

Angels, when the sun is hottest
May be seen the sands among,
Stooping—plucking—sighing—flying—
Parched the flowers they bear along.

Howard Schwartz

The Angel of Conception

(9th century Babylon)

Among the angels there is one who serves as the midwife of souls. This is Lailah, the angel of conception. When the time has come for conception, Lailah seeks out a certain soul hidden in the Garden of Eden and commands it to enter the seed. The soul is always reluctant, for it still remembers the pain of being born, and it prefers to remain pure. But Lailah compels the soul to obey, and that is how new life comes into being.

While the infant grows in the womb, Lailah watches over it, reading the unborn child the history of its soul. All the while a light shines upon the head of the child, by which it sees from one end of the world to the other. And Lailah shows the child the rewards of the Garden of Eden, as well as the punishments of Gehenna. But when the time has come to be born, the angel extinguishes the light and brings forth the child into the world, and as it is brought forth, it cries. Then Lailah lightly strikes the newborn above the lip, causing it to forget all it has learned. And that is the origin of this mark, which everyone bears.

Indeed, Lailah is a guardian angel who watches over us all of our days. And when the time has come to take leave of this world, it is Lailah who leads us to the World to Come.

Traditional African Myth

The Spirit in the Tree

Long ago there lived a farmer and his beautiful daughter. The farmer's wife had died, and he was full of sorrow for she was a good and kindly woman and he knew his young daughter longed for a mother's love. In due time he took another wife, but instead of loving the young girl as her own, the woman treated the farmer's daughter cruelly. The child was rarely given enough to eat, and was made to spend hours toiling under the scorching sun. Often she would slip away to her mother's grave, where she would sit, weeping.

One day, as she sat by the grave, she saw a small green shoot coming up from the earth where her mother was buried. The next day the shoot was a little bigger. Every day the girl went to look, and every day it had grown some more. Very soon it had become a sturdy young tree, its branches bent low with succulent fruit. Day after day, sitting in the shade of the branches, the girl picked the fruit and ate. Every now and then she was sure she could hear her mother's spirit rustling through the leaves.

It was not long before the stepmother noticed that the girl was looking well and more beautiful. "How can this be?" she wondered. The following morning she followed the girl to the graveside. When she saw the tree, she rushed back to her husband and demanded the tree be felled for firewood. She would not rest until he agreed, and so the tree was cut down. But its branches would not burn, and it was

left, lifeless, by the side of the grave.

Sad and hungry once more, the girl sat by the tree and wept. Suddenly she stopped. There, before her eyes, a pumpkin was growing out of her mother's grave. Larger and larger it grew, and again the girl was certain she heard her mother's spirit whispering above her. She broke a piece of the fruit and ate.

Every morning the girl returned to the grave, and every morning there was a fresh pumpkin awaiting her. Soon her health returned and she grew more beautiful.

Again, the stepmother noticed the change and followed the child to the graveside. When she saw the pumpkin, she was filled with fury. Late that night, when her husband and stepdaughter were asleep, she crept out and, with an ax, splintered the pumpkin into a thousand pieces. Then she chopped at the earth until all the roots had been destroyed.

When the girl discovered what had happened, she was grief stricken. She lay by the grave, her tears falling onto the parched earth. Just then she heard a gentle trickling and saw, out of the grave, a small spring bubbling. Its water was cold and refreshing, and the girl was certain she could hear her mother calling to her as the water welled up and rippled beside her. She cupped her hands and drank.

It was not long before the stepmother discovered the spring. In blind rage she again stole out in the depth of night. Taking a shovel, she dug until the spring was filled in, the earth on the grave once more parched and barren.

Long days passed and the girl would sit on her mother's grave, mourning. One evening, as the setting sun filled the horizon, the air cooled and the animals came out to seek water; the girl saw a young hunter walking toward her from the bush. He came up to her and, seeing the tree lying by the grave, its leaves withered and scorched, asked if he might cut some wood to make arrows.

At first the girl hesitated. Sitting under that tree, she had first heard her mother's spirit. She was unsure. Then she heard her mother again, her spirit rustling even through the dying leaves. Comforted, she agreed to let the hunter cut a small branch.

He sat down beside her and fashioned arrow after arrow with his knife. All night long they sat and talked, and the girl told him of her unhappiness. By the time the sun began to rise, the hunter had fallen in love with this beautiful girl and vowed to marry her and bring her happiness. That morning he went to ask the farmer for his daughter's hand in marriage.

The farmer agreed, but only on condition that the hunter kill a herd of buffalo. The hunter had never before killed so many buffalo but, undaunted, he set out with his new arrows in his belt. All day he tracked the herd until they stopped by a water hole. Then, taking arrow after arrow, he aimed and fired, and one by one the beasts fell to the ground.

The hunter returned to the farmer to claim his bride, and the buffalo were carried back for the wedding feast. As the girl looked forward to a life of happiness, she was sure she could hear her mother's spirit whispering words of joy around her.

Traditional

African

Myth

Edgar   Allan   Poe

İSRAFEL

In Heaven a spirit doth dwell
  'Whose heart-strings are a lute';
None sing so wildly well
As the angel Israfel,
And the giddy stars (so legends tell),
Ceasing their hymns, attend the spell
  Of his voice, all mute.

And they say (the starry choir
  And the other listening things)
That Israfeli's fire
Is owing to that lyre
  By which he sits and sings—
The trembling living wire
  Of those unusual strings.

If I could dwell
Where Israfel
  Hath dwelt, and he where I,
He might not sing so wildly well
  A mortal melody,
While a bolder note than this might swell
  From my lyre within the sky.

Sophy Burnham

THE ANGELS OF MONS

I have heard that during World War II, some people claimed the Allied victory was due to angels fighting on their side. But the most dramatic of the war stories, a Song of Roland of this age, concerns the angels at Mons in Belgium. The visitation occurred between the twenty-sixth and the twenty-eighth of August, 1914, during the first engagements of World War I. The French and British were retreating toward Paris, overpowered by the German guns. This was nothing like the slaughter that took place later in this war, when the average life expectancy of a British officer at the front was said to be twenty minutes, but it was nonetheless a sad and bloody retreat.

Then the stories began to dribble in—that the men had seen angels on the field. Nothing was clear about the tales.

The French had seen the archangel Saint Michael (or was it Saint Joan?) bareheaded, clad in golden armor and seated on a white horse, brandishing a sword. To the British it was Saint George, springing out of a yellow mist, "a tall man with yellow hair in golden armor, on a white horse, holding his sword up, and his mouth open, crying *Victory!*" And it was not just one or two men who saw this. The nurse in one hospital reported that she and her fellow nurses heard the tale again and again from the wounded, with men from both nationalities asking repeatedly for medals or pictures of either Saint Michael or Saint George. What

the nurses found most curious was the air of exaltation or serene joy that accompanied these dying men.

One patient said that at a critical period in the retreat from Mons he saw "an angel with outstretched wings, like a luminous cloud," between the advancing Germans and themselves, and at that moment the onslaught of the Germans slackened.

Another reported a "strange light, which seemed to be quite distinctly outlined and was not a reflection of the moon. . . . The light became brighter and I could see quite distinctly three shapes, one in the centre having what looked like outspread wings, the other two were not so large, but were quite plainly distinct from the centre one. They appeared to have a long, loose-hanging garment of a golden tint, and they were above the German line facing us."

A year later rumors appeared from the German side: that at a certain moment the men were "absolutely powerless to proceed . . . and their horses turned sharply round and fled . . . and nothing could stop them." Back in Germany a severe reprimand was allegedly given to this regiment. But the German soldiers claimed they saw that the Allied lines were held by thousands of troops —"thousands," although in reality it was a thin line of two regiments, with men stationed fifteen yards apart or straggling down the roads in disorderly retreat.

Had the soldiers seen something? Who can tell? The stories cannot be confirmed. In some cases it was a single angel, in others several, hovering over the battlefield, in others a ghostly troop of cavalry riding guard for the retreating men.

Meanwhile back in England, a journalist, Arthur Machen, had been so moved when he heard on the radio the news of the retreat from Mons that he had written a short story. Entitled "The Bowmen," it appeared in the *London Evening News* September 14, 1914, three weeks after the event, and recounted how the retreating men had seen an apparition of "shining" medieval soldiers, phantom bowmen from the fifteenth-century battle of Agincourt, located right near Mons.

When the stories of angels began to sift back home, Machen thought word had picked up from his story. He spent considerable time trying to persuade people he had made it up—Untrue! No apparitions had appeared!

Yet the stories persisted. He never succeeded in quashing the tales.

One man suggested that the apparitions were the souls of the just-dead, still hovering near their comrades. Others said the tales were all untrue, the product of fever and fatigue in a war where the nurses in one field hospital were working forty-five hours without sleep, and, as the horse-drawn carts of the wounded rolled in, they pulled the living out from under corpses already cold. Some people say that the stories of angels resulted from the mass hysteria besetting an army of a hundred thousand that had set out only days before expecting instant victory and instead saw fifteen thousand men lost in the first engagement; and Machen, of course, egoistically took credit for the tales derived from his story of fifteenth-century longbowmen who covered the army's retreat.

But some people believe that angels were at Mons.

S o p h y

B u r n h a m

Mark   Twain

FROM CAPTAIN STORMFIELD'S
VISIT TO HEAVEN

The very next instant a voice I knew sung out in a business kind of a way—

"A harp and a hymn-book, pair of wings and a halo, size 13, for Cap'n Eli Stormfield, of San Francisco!—make him out a clean bill of health, and let him in."

I opened my eyes. Sure enough, it was a Pi Ute Injun I used to know in Tulare County; mighty good fellow—I remembered being at his funeral, which consisted of him being burnt and the other Injuns gauming their faces with his ashes and howling like wild cats. He was powerful glad to see me, and you may make up your mind I was just as glad to see him, and felt that I was in the right kind of a heaven at last.

Just as far as your eye could reach, there was swarms of clerks, running and bustling around, tricking out thousands of Yanks and Mexicans and English and Arabs, and all sorts of people in their new outfits; and when they gave me my kit and I put on my halo and I took a look in the glass, I could have jumped over a house for joy, I was so happy. "Now *this* is something like!" says I. "Now," says I, "I'm all right—show me a cloud."

Inside of fifteen minutes I was a mile on my way towards the cloud-banks and about a million people along with me. Most of us tried to fly, but some got crippled and nobody made a success of it. So we concluded to walk, for the present, till we had had some wing practice.

We begun to meet swarms of folks who were coming back. Some had harps and nothing else; some had hymn-books and nothing else; some had nothing at all; all of them looked meek and uncomfortable; one young fellow hadn't anything left but his halo, and he was carrying that in his hand; all of a sudden he offered it to me and says—

"Will you hold it for me a minute?"

Then he disappeared in the crowd. I went on. A woman asked me to hold her palm branch, and then *she* disappeared. A girl got me to hold her harp for her, and by George, *she* disappeared; and so on and so on, till I was about loaded down to the guards. Then comes a smiling old gentleman and asked me to hold *his* things. I swabbed off the perspiration and says, pretty tart—

"I'll have to get you to excuse me, my friend,—*I* ain't no hat-rack."

About this time I begun to run across piles of those traps, lying in the road. I just quietly dumped my extra cargo along with them. I looked around, and, Peters, that whole nation that was following me were loaded down the same as I'd been. The return crowd had got them to hold their things a minute, you see. They all dumped their loads, too, and we went on.

When I found myself perched on a cloud, with a million other people, I never felt so good in my life. Says I, "Now this is according to the promises; I've been having my doubts, but now I am in heaven, sure enough." I gave my palm branch a wave or two, for luck, and then I tautened up my harp-strings and struck in. Well, Peters, you can't imagine anything like the row we made. It was grand to listen to, and made a body thrill all over, but there was considerable many tunes going on at once, and that was a drawback to the harmony, you understand; and then there was a lot of Injun tribes, and they kept up such another war-whooping that they kind of took the tuck out of the music. By and by I quit performing, and judged I'd take a rest. There was quite a nice mild old gentleman sitting next me, and I noticed he didn't take a hand; I encouraged him, but he said he was naturally bashful, and was

Mark

Twain

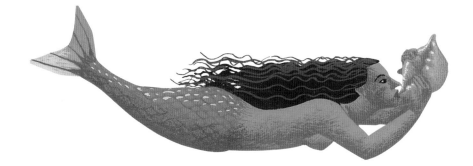

afraid to try before so many people. By and by the old gentleman said he never could seem to enjoy music somehow. The fact was, I was beginning to feel the same way; but I didn't say anything. Him and I had a considerable long silence, then, but of course it warn't noticeable in that place. After about sixteen or seventeen hours, during which I played and sung a little, now and then—always the same tune, because I didn't know any other—I laid down my harp and begun to fan myself with my palm branch. Then we both got to sighing pretty regular. Finally, says he—

"Don't you know any tune but the one you've been pegging at all day?"

"Not another blessed one," says I.

"Don't you reckon you could learn another one?" says he.

"Never," says I; "I've tried to, but I couldn't manage it."

"It's a long time to hang to the one—eternity, you know."

"Don't break my heart," says I; "I'm getting low-spirited enough already."

After another long silence, says he—

"Are you glad to be here?"

Says I, "Old man, I'll be frank with you. This *ain't* just as near my idea of bliss as I thought it was going to be, when I used to go to church."

Says he, "What do you say to knocking off and calling it half a day?"

"That's me," says I. "I never wanted to get off watch so bad in my life."

So we started. Millions were coming to the cloud-bank all the time, happy and hosannahing; millions were leaving it all the time, looking mighty quiet, I tell you. We laid for the newcomers, and pretty soon I'd got them to hold all my things a minute, and then I was a free man again and most outrageously happy. Just then I ran across old Sam Bartlett, who had been dead a long time, and stopped to have a talk with him. Says I—

"Now tell me—is this to go on forever? Ain't there anything else for a change?"

Says he—

"I'll set you right on that point very quick. People take the figurative language of the Bible and the allegories for literal, and the first thing they ask for when they get here is a halo and a harp, and so on. Nothing that's harmless and reasonable is refused a body here, if he asks it in the right spirit. So they are outfitted with these things without a word. They go and sing and play just about one day, and that's the last you'll ever see them in the choir. They don't need anybody to tell them that that sort of thing wouldn't make a heaven—at least not a heaven that a sane man could stand a week and remain sane. That cloud-bank is placed where the noise can't disturb the old inhabitants, and so there ain't any harm in letting everybody get up there and cure himself as soon as he comes.

"Now you just remember this—heaven is as blissful and lovely as it can be; but it's just the busiest place you ever heard of. There ain't any idle people here after the first day. Singing hymns and waving palm branches through all eternity is pretty when you hear about it in the pulpit, but it's as poor a way to put in valuable time as a body could contrive. It would just make a heaven of warbling ignoramuses, don't you see? Eternal Rest sounds comforting in the pulpit, too. Well, you try it once, and see how heavy time will hang on your hands. Why, Stormfield, a man like you, that had been active and stirring all his life, would go mad in six months in a heaven where he hadn't anything to do. Heaven is the very last place to come to rest in—and don't you be afraid to bet on that!"

Says I—

"Sam, I'm as glad to hear it as I thought I'd be sorry. I'm glad I come, now."

Black Rook in Rainy Weather

On the stiff twig up there

Hunches a wet black rook

Arranging and rearranging its feathers in the rain.

I do not expect a miracle

Or an accident

To set the sight on fire

In my eye, nor seek

Any more in the desultory weather some design,

But let spotted leaves fall as they fall,

Without ceremony, or portent.

Although, I admit, I desire,

Occasionally, some backtalk

From the mute sky, I can't honestly complain:

A certain minor light may still

Lean incandescent

Out of kitchen table or chair
As if a celestial burning took
Possession of the most obtuse objects now and then—
Thus hallowing an interval
Otherwise inconsequent

By bestowing largesse, honor,
One might say love. At any rate, I now walk
Wary (for it could happen
Even in this dull, ruinous landscape); skeptical,
Yet politic; ignorant

Of whatever angel may choose to flare
Suddenly at my elbow. I only know that a rook
Ordering its black feathers can so shine
As to seize my senses, haul
My eyelids up, and grant

A brief respite from fear
Of total neutrality. With luck,
Trekking stubborn through this season
Of fatigue, I shall
Patch together a content

Sylvia

Plath

Of sorts. Miracles occur,
If you care to call those spasmodic
Tricks of radiance miracles. The wait's begun again,
The long wait for the angel,
For that rare, random descent.

R u d y   W i e b e

The Angel of the Tar Sands

Spring had most certainly, finally, come. The morning drive to the plant from Fort McMurray was so dazzling with fresh green against the heavy spruce, the air so unearthly bright that it swallowed the smoke from the candy-striped chimneys as if it did not exist. Which is just lovely, the superintendent thought, cut out all the visible crud, shut up the environmentalists, and he went into his neat office (with the river view with islands) humming, "Alberta blue, Alberta blue, the taste keeps—" but did not get his tan golfing jacket off before he was interrupted. Not by the radio-telephone, by Tak the day operator on Number Two Bucket in person, walking past the secretary without stopping.

"What the hell?" the superintendent said, quickly annoyed.

"I ain't reporting this on no radio," Tak's imperturbable Japanese-Canadian face was tense, "if them reporters hear about this one they—"

"You scrape out *another* buffalo skeleton, for god's sake?"

"No, it's maybe a dinosaur this time, one of them—"

But the superintendent, swearing, was already out the door yelling for Bertha who was always on stand-by now with her spade. If one of the three nine-storey-high bucketwheels stopped turning for an hour the plant dropped capacity, but another archaeological leak could stop every bit of production for a month while bifocalled professors stuck their noses . . . the jeep leaped along the track beside the

conveyor belt running a third empty already and in three minutes he had Bertha with her long-handled spade busy on the face of the fifty-foot cliff that Number Two had been gnawing out. A shape emerged, quickly.

"What the . . ." staring, the superintendent could not find his ritual words, ". . . is that?"

"When the bucket hit the corner of it," Tak said, "I figured hey, that's the bones of a—"

"That's not just bone, it's . . . skin and. . . ." The superintendent could not say the word.

"Wings," Bertha said it for him, digging her spade in with steady care. "That's wings, like you'd expect on an angel."

For that's what it was, plain as the day now, tucked tight into the oozing black cliff, an angel. Tak had seen only a corner of bones sheared clean but now that Bertha had it more uncovered they saw the manlike head through one folded-over pair of wings and the manlike legs, feet through another pair, very gaunt, the film of feathers and perhaps skin so thin and engrained with tarry sand that at first it was impossible to notice anything except the white bones inside them. The third pair of wings was pressed flat by the sand at a very awkward angle, it must have been painful—

"The middle two," Bertha said, trying to brush the sticky sand aside with her hand, carefully, "is what it flies with."

"Wouldn't it . . . he . . . fly with all six . . . six . . ." The superintendent stopped, overwhelmed by the unscientific shape uncovered there so blatantly.

"You can look it up," Bertha said with a sideways glance at his ignorance, "Isaiah chapter six."

But then she gagged too for the angel had moved. Not one of them was touching it, that was certain, but it had moved irrefutably. As they watched, stunned, the wings unfolded bottom and top, a head emerged, turned, and they saw the fierce hoary lineaments of an ancient man. His mouth all encrusted with tar pulled open and out came a sound. A long, throat-clearing streak of sound. They staggered back, fell; the superintendent found himself on his knees staring up at the shape which wasn't really very tall, it just seemed immensely broad and overwhelming, the three sets of wings now sweeping back and forth as if loosening up in some seraphic 5BX plan. The voice rumbled like thunder, steadily on.

"Well," muttered Tak, "whatever it is, it sure ain't talking Japanese."

The superintendent suddenly saw himself as an altar boy, the angel suspended above him there and bits of words rose to his lips: "*Pax vobis . . . cem . . . cum,*" he ventured, but the connections were lost in the years, "*Magnifi . . . cat . . . ave Mar . . .*"

The obsidian eyes of the angel glared directly at him and it roared something, dreadfully. Bertha laughed aloud.

"Forget the popish stuff," she said. "It's talking Hutterite, Hutterite German."

"Wha . . ." The superintendent had lost all words; he was down to syllables only.

"I left the colony. . . ." But then she was too busy listening. The angel kept on speaking, non-stop as if words had been plugged up inside for eons, and its hands (it had only two of them, in the usual place at the ends of two arms) brushed double over its bucket-damaged shoulder and that appeared restored, whole just like the other, while it brushed the soil and tarry sand from its wings, flexing the middle ones again and again because they obviously had suffered much from their position.

"Ber . . . Ber . . ." the superintendent said. Finally he looked at Tak, pleading for a voice.

"What's it saying," Tak asked her, "Bertha, please Bertha?"

She was listening with overwhelming intensity; there was nothing in this world but to hear. Tak touched her shoulder, shook her, but she did not notice. Suddenly the angel stopped speaking; it was studying her.

"I . . . I can't. . . ." Bertha confessed to it at last, "I can understand every word you . . . every word, but I can't say, I've forgotten. . . ."

In its silence the angel looked at her; slowly its expression changed. It might have been showing pity, though of course that is really difficult to tell with angels. Then it folded its lower wings over its feet, its upper wings over its face, and with an ineffable movement of its giant middle wings it rose, straight upward into the blue sky. They bent back staring after it, and in a moment it had vanished in light.

"O dear god," Bertha murmured after a time. "Our Elder always said they spoke Hutterite in heaven."

They three contemplated each other and they saw in each other's eyes the dread, the abrupt tearing sensation of doubt. Had they seen . . . and as one they looked at the sand cliff still oozing tar, the spade leaning against it. Beside the hole where Bertha had dug: the shape of the angel, indelible. Bertha was the first to get up.

"I quit," she said. "Right this minute."

"Of course, I understand." The superintendent was on his feet. "Tak, run your bucket through there, get it going quick."

"Okay," Tak said heavily. "You're the boss."

"It doesn't matter how fast you do it," Bertha said to the superintendent but she was watching Tak trudge into the shadow of the giant wheel. "It was there, we saw it."

And at her words the superintendent had a vision. He saw like an opened book the immense curves of the Athabasca River swinging through wilderness down from the glacial pinnacles of the Rocky Mountains and across Alberta and joined by the Berland and the McLeod and the Pembina and the Pelican and the Christina and the Clearwater and the Firebag rivers, and all the surface of the earth was gone, the Tertiary and the Lower Cretaceous layers of strata had been ripped away and the thousands of square miles of black bituminous sand were exposed, laid open, slanting down into the molten centre of the earth, *O miserere, miserere*, the words sang in his head and he felt their meaning though he could not have explained them, much less remembered Psalm 51, and after a time he could open his eyes and lift his head. The huge plant, he knew every bolt and pipe, still sprawled between him and the river; the brilliant air still swallowed the smoke from all the red-striped chimneys as if it did not exist, and he knew that through a thousand secret openings the oil ran there, gurgling in each precisely numbered pipe and jointure, sweet and clear like golden brown honey.

Tak was beside the steel ladder, about to start the long climb into the machine. Bertha touched his shoulder and they both looked up.

"Next time you'll recognize it," she said happily. "And then it'll talk Japanese."

85

R u d y

W i e b e

R o b e r t   H u l l

The Last Journey

(Native American Myth)

It was the summer's end, the time when sadness crosses the land in lengthening shadows from the mountains, and thistledown floats along the rivers.

Wahu had been a fine hunter. He had always caught enough food for his family, and never been wearied by the endless trails over the mountains or the long cold days on the river. But his strength was leaving him. He could not hunt as he used to. Now, except for his dog, Wahu was alone. His wife had died, and his children lived in distant valleys and villages with their own families. He didn't have the strength to visit them again.

He would talk to his dog sometimes, but mainly Wahu spoke with the long shadows, and the voices that came to him from the mists that hung in the valley in the evening. The voices came to him from times that had passed, from the dear ones who had gone, and the close friends of his childhood.

Wahu could no longer take an interest in the present, and knew that it would soon be time for him to begin his last journey. He made ready his canoe. He took out his worn paddle, splintered from the many rocks the water had surged round in his youth.

He thought of the times he had made the journey with friends. He could almost hear their laughter on the water. He thought of the dawns and sunsets he had seen on the river. He remembered the times he'd seen elk standing at the water's edge, and the salmon that had leapt glimmering by him. This was a journey he would make alone, without friends or laughter, and he would not stop to fish, or to make camp and wait for the next dawn to rise.

It was time to begin. He pushed off in the early morning from the small beach where he had always moored his canoe, and looked round once, to see the sun shining in the pine-tops over the clearing where he had built his lodge long ago, and down through the coiling river-mist where he drifted now.

The water was still and dark.

He could see no fish. Behind him, his dog stood in the shallows, waiting for the canoe to turn round and come back to fetch her. Instead, there was only the wave of Wahu's arm as the canoe slowly wound out of sight.

For hours the trail of the canoe made a long calm "V" on the water. The sun rose to its noon height, then fell slowly across the long afternoon. The shadows lengthened and the air became cool. Wahu would soon be able to hear the thunder of the white water. He had never been this far, but he had heard of the white water that foamed and spilled between high rocks. The sound foretold the end of his journey.

The tall rocks came into sight. They were at the entrance to the road to the Last Hunting Ground. Here he had to pause. He drove his canoe gently into the shallows. Two shadowy figures stepped forward.

"Are you alone?" said one. "It is sad to travel to the Last Hunting Ground unaccompanied."

"Yes I am alone."

But he was not. His dog had followed him all the way, sometimes swimming behind the canoe, sometimes following the trail as it wound along the bank. At that moment she pulled herself out of the water, and shook herself. She trotted over and jumped into the canoe. The shadowy figures pushed them off, towards the white water. They had no need for a paddle now. The spirits would keep the canoe riding clear of the rocks, until they were into the Long White Water of the Sky, drifting towards the Last Hunting Ground.

A l l a n   G u r g a n u s

It Had Wings

Find a little yellow side street house. Put an older woman in it. Dress her in that
tatty favorite robe, pull her slippers up before the sink, have her doing dishes, gazing nowhere—at her own backyard. Gazing everywhere. Something falls outside,
loud. One damp thwunk into new grass. A meteor? She herself (retired from selling
formal clothes at Wanamaker's, she herself—a widow and the mother of three scattered sons, she herself alone at home a lot these days) goes onto tiptoe, leans across
a sinkful of suds, sees—out near her picnic table, something nude, white, overly-
long. It keeps shivering. Both wings seem damaged.

"No way," she says. It appears human. Yes, it is a male one. It's face up and,
you can tell, it is extremely male (uncircumcised). This old woman, pushing eighty,
a history of aches, uses, fun—now presses one damp hand across her eyes. Blaming
strain, the luster of new cataracts, she looks again. Still, it rests there on a bright air
mattress of its own wings. Outer feathers are tough quills, broad at bottom as row-
boat oars. The whole left wing bends far under. It looks hurt.

The widow, sighing, takes up her blue willow mug of heated milk. Shaking her
head, muttering, she carries it out back. She moves so slow because: arthritis. It crit-
icizes every step. It asks about the mug she holds, Do you really need this?

• • •

She stoops, creaky, beside what can only be a young angel, unconscious. Quick, she checks overhead, ready for what?—some TV news crew in a helicopter? She sees only a sky of the usual size, a Tuesday sky stretched between weekends. She allows herself to touch this thing's white forehead. She gets a mild electric shock. Then, odd, her tickled finger joints stop aching. They've hurt so long. A practical person, she quickly cures her other hand. The angel grunts but sounds pleased. His temperature's a hundred and fifty, easy—but for him, this seems somehow normal. "Poor thing," she says, and—careful—pulls his heavy curly head into her lap. The head hums like a phone knocked off its cradle. She scans for neighbors, hoping they'll come out, wishing they wouldn't, both.

"Look, will warm milk help?" She pours some down him. Her wrist brushes angel skin. Which pulls the way an ice tray begs whatever touches it. A thirty-year pain leaves her, enters him. Even her liver spots are lightening. He grunts with pleasure, soaking up all of it. Bold, she presses her worst hip deep into crackling feathers. The hip has been half numb since a silly fall last February. All stiffness leaves her. He goes, "Unhh." Her griefs seem to fatten him like vitamins. Bolder, she whispers private woes: the Medicare cuts, the sons too casual by half, the daughters-in-law not bad but not so great. These woes seem ended. "Nobody'll believe. Still, tell me some of it." She tilts nearer. Both his eyes stay shut but his voice, like clicks from a million crickets pooled, goes, "We're just another army. We all look alike—we didn't, before. It's not what you expect. We miss this other. Don't count on the next. Notice things here. We are just another army."

"Oh," she says.

Nodding, she feels limber now, sure as any girl of twenty. Admiring her unspeckled hands, she helps him rise. Wings serve as handles. Kneeling on damp ground, she watches him go staggering toward her barbecue pit. Awkward for an athlete, really awkward for an angel, the poor thing climbs up there, wobbly. Standing, he is handsome, but as a vase is handsome. When he turns this way, she sees his eyes. They're silver, each reflects her: a speck, pink, on green green grass.

She now fears he plans to take her up, as thanks. She presses both palms flat to dirt, says, "The house is finally paid off. —Not just yet," and smiles.

Suddenly he's infinitely infinitely more so. Silvery. Raw. Gleaming like a sunny monument, a clock. Each wing puffs, independent. Feathers sort and shuffle like three hundred packs of playing cards. Out flings either arm; knees dip low. Then up and off he shoves, one solemn grunt. Machete swipes cross her backyard, breezes cool her upturned face. Six feet overhead, he falters, whips in makeshift circles, manages to hold aloft, then go shrub-high, gutter-high. He avoids a messy tangle of phone lines now rocking from the wind of him. "Go, go," the widow, grinning, points the way. "Do. Yeah, good." He signals back at her, open-mouthed and left down here. First a glinting man-shaped kite, next an oblong of aluminum in sun. Now a new moon shrunk to decent star, one fleck, fleck's memory: usual Tuesday sky.

She kneels, panting, happier and frisky. She is hungry but must first rush over and tell Lydia next door. Then she pictures Lydia's worry lines bunching. Lydia will maybe phone the missing sons: "Come right home. Your Mom's inventing . . . company."

Maybe other angels have dropped into other Elm Street backyards? Behind fences, did neighbors help earlier hurt ones? Folks keep so much of the best stuff quiet, don't they.

Palms on knees, she stands, wirier. This retired saleswoman was the formal-gowns adviser to ten mayors' wives. She spent sixty years of nine-to-five on her feet. Scuffing indoors, now, staring down at terry slippers, she decides, "Got to wash these next week." Can a person who's just sighted her first angel already be mulling about laundry? Yes. The world is like that.

From her sink, she sees her own blue willow mug out there in the grass. It rests in muddy ruts where the falling body struck so hard. A neighbor's collie keeps barking. (It saw!) Okay. This happened. "So," she says.

And plunges hands into dishwater, still warm. Heat usually helps her achy joints feel agile. But fingers don't even hurt now. Her bad hip doesn't pinch one bit. And yet, sad, they all will. By suppertime, they will again remind her what usual suffering means. To her nimble underwater hands, the widow, staring straight ahead, announces, "I helped. He flew off stronger. I really egged him on. Like any-body would've, really. Still, it was me. I'm not just somebody in a house. I'm not just somebody alone in a house. I'm not just somebody else alone in a house."

Feeling more herself, she finishes the breakfast dishes. In time for lunch. This old woman should be famous for all she has been through—today's angel, her years in sales, the sons and friends—she should be famous for her life. She knows things, she has seen so much. She's not famous.

Still, the lady keeps gazing past her kitchen café curtains, she keeps studying her

own small tidy yard. An Anchor fence, the picnic table, a barbecue pit, new Bermuda grass. Hands braced on her sink's cool edge, she tips nearer a bright window.

She seems to be expecting something, expecting something decent. Her kitchen clock is ticking. That dog still barks to calm itself. And she keeps staring out: nowhere, everywhere. Spots on her hands are darkening again. And yet, she whispers, "I'm right here, ready. Ready for more."

Can you guess why this old woman's chin is lifted? Why does she breathe as if to show exactly how it's done? Why should both her shoulders, usually quite bent, brace so square just now?

She is guarding the world.

Only, nobody knows.

Flannery O'Connor

Letter to "A,"
17th January 1956

I don't want to be any angel but my relations with them have improved over a period of time. They weren't always even speakable. I went to the Sisters to school for the first 6 years or so . . . at their hands I developed something the Freudians have not named—anti-angel aggression, call it. From 8 to 12 years it was my habit to seclude myself in a locked room every so often and with a fierce (and evil) face, whirl around in a circle with my fists knotted, socking the angel. This was the guardian angel with which the Sisters assured us we were all equipped. He never left you. My dislike of him was poisonous. I'm sure I even kicked at him and landed on the floor. You couldn't hurt an angel but I would have been happy to know I had dirtied his feathers—I conceived of him in feathers. Anyway, the Lord removed this fixation from me by His Merciful Kindness and I have not been troubled by it since. In fact I forgot that angels existed until a couple of years ago the *Catholic Worker* sent me a card on which was printed a prayer to St. Raphael. . . . The prayer asks St. Raphael to guide us to the province of joy so that we may not be ignorant of the concerns of our true country. All this led me to find out eventually what angels were, or anyway what they were not. And what they are not is a big comfort to me . . .

Donald   Barthelme

On Angels

The death of God left the angels in a strange position. They were overtaken suddenly by a fundamental question. One can attempt to imagine the moment. How did they *look* at the instant the question invaded them, flooding the angelic consciousness, taking hold with terrifying force? The question was, "What are angels?"

New to questioning, unaccustomed to terror, unskilled in aloneness, the angels (we assume) fell into despair.

The question of what angels "are" has a considerable history. Swedenborg, for example, talked to a great many angels and faithfully recorded what they told him. Angels look like human beings, Swedenborg says. "That angels are human forms, or men, has been seen by me a thousand times." And again: "From all of my experience, which is now of many years, I am able to state that angels are wholly men in form, having faces, eyes, ears, bodies, arms, hands, and feet . . ." But a man cannot see angels with his bodily eyes, only with the eyes of the spirit.

Swedenborg has a great deal more to say about angels, all of the highest interest: that no angel is ever permitted to stand behind another and look at the back of his head, for this would disturb the influx of good and truth from the Lord; that angels have the east, where the Lord is seen as a sun, always before their eyes; and that angels are clothed according to their intelligence. "Some of the most intelligent

have garments that blaze as if with flame, others have garments that glisten as if with light; the less intelligent have garments that are glistening white or white without the effulgence; and the still less intelligent have garments of various colors. But the angels of the inmost heaven are not clothed."

All of this (presumably) no longer obtains.

Gustav Davidson, in his useful *Dictionary of Angels*, has brought together much of what is known about them. Their names are called: the angel Elubatel, the angel Friagne, the angel Gaap, the angel Hatiphas (genius of finery), the angel Murmur (a fallen angel), the angel Mqttro, the angel Or, the angel Rash, the angel Sandalphon (taller than a five hundred years' journey on foot), the angel Smat. Davidson distinguishes categories: Angels of Quaking, who surround the heavenly throne; Masters of Howling and Lords of Shouting, whose work is praise; messengers, mediators, watchers, warners. Davidson's *Dictionary* is a very large book; his bibliography lists more than eleven hundred items.

The former angelic consciousness has been most beautifully described by Joseph Lyons (in a paper titled *The Psychology of Angels*, published in 1957). Each angel, Lyons says, knows all that there is to know about himself and every other angel. "No angel could ever ask a question, because questioning proceeds out of a situation of not knowing, and of being in some way aware of not knowing. An angel cannot be curious; he has nothing to be curious about. He cannot wonder. Knowing all that there is to know, the world of possible knowledge must appear to him as an ordered set of facts which is completely behind him, completely fixed and certain and within his grasp . . ."

But this, too, no longer obtains.

It is a curiosity of writing about angels that, very often, one turns out to be writing about men. The themes are twinned. Thus one finally learns that Lyons, for example, is really writing not about angels but about schizophrenics—thinking about men by invoking angels. And this holds true of much other writing on the subject—a point, we may assume, that was not lost on the angels when they began considering their new relation to the cosmos, when the analogues (is an angel more like a quetzal or more like a man? or more like music?) were being handed about.

We may further assume that some attempt was made at self definition by function. An angel is what he does. Thus it was necessary to investigate possible new roles (you are reminded that this is impure speculation). After the lamentation had gone on for hundreds and hundreds of whatever the angels use for time, an angel proposed that lamentation be the function of angels eternally, as adoration was formerly. The mode of lamentation would be silence, in contrast to the unceasing chanting of Glorias that had been their former employment. But it is not in the nature of angels to be silent.

A counterproposal was that the angels affirm chaos. There were to be five great proofs of the existence of chaos, of which the first was the absence of God. The other four could surely be located. The work of definition and explication could, if done nicely enough, occupy the angels forever, as the contrary work has occupied human theologians. But there is not much enthusiasm for chaos among the angels.

The most serious because most radical proposal considered by the angels was refusal—that they would remove themselves from being, not be. The tremendous dignity that would accrue to the angels by this act was felt to be a manifestation of spiritual pride. Refusal was refused.

There were other suggestions, more subtle and complicated, less so, none overwhelmingly attractive.

I saw a famous angel on television; his garments glistened as if with light. He talked about the situation of angels now. Angels, he said, are like men *in some ways*. The problem of adoration is felt to be central. He said that for a time the angels had tried adoring each other, as we do, but had found it, finally, "not enough." He said they are continuing to search for a new principle.

99

Donald

Barthelme

Anne Bradstreet

The Flesh and the Spirit

100

Mine Eye doth pierce the heavens, and see
What is Invisible to thee.
My garments are not silk nor gold,
Nor such like trash which Earth doth hold,
But Royal Robes I shall have on,
More glorious than the glistring Sun;
My Crown not Diamonds, Pearls, and Gold,
But such as Angels heads infold.
The City where I hope to dwell,
There's none on Earth can Parallel:
The stately Walls both high and strong,
Are made of pretious Jasper stone;
The Gates of Pearl, both rich and clear,
And Angels are for Porters there;
The Streets thereof transparent gold,
Such as no Eye did e're behold;
A Chrystal River there doth run,
Which doth proceed from the Lamb's Throne.

M a l c o l m   G o d w i n

The Archangels

Most people can name at least two or three Archangels. Of all the angelic orders these justifiably have the greatest claim to fame. The seven angels who stand before God in Revelations are usually interpreted as the Archangels. The Koran of Islam only recognizes four and actually names but two—Jibril (Gabriel) and Michael. While Christian and Jewish sources agree on the number seven, there is an unholy debate as to who they might actually be. Four names which do however appear regularly are: Michael, Gabriel, Rapha-el and Uri-el. The other three candidates are traditionally chosen from Metatron, Remi-el, Sari-el, Ana-el, Ragu-el and Razi-el.

Dionysius tells us that Archangels are "Messengers which carry Divine Decrees." They are considered the most important intercessionaries between God and humans and it is they who command the legions of Heaven in their constant battle with the Sons of Darkness.

Archangel Micha-el

His name means "who is as God." In most Christian lore he is the "Greatest." In fact he and Gabriel are the only two actually mentioned in the Old Testament at all, save for Raphael who introduces himself in the Catholic *Book of Tobit*.

Originally Michael was a Chaldean deity but since those ancient days his exploits have captured the popular imagination far more than any other angel. Many of his deeds are also attributed to the other Archangels. It is a measure of Micha-el's popularity that this should occur.

In one account he is said to have wiped out, single-handed and overnight, a hundred and eighty-five thousand men from the army of the Assyrian king, Sennercherib, who was threatening Jerusalem in 701 B.C. Michael is said to have stayed the hand of Abraham who was about to sacrifice his son Isaac. According to Jewish lore it is Michael who appeared to Moses in the midst of a burning bush and who appears again in the burial episode, where he disputes the possession of the body of the old patriarch with Satan. It is Michael who will descend from heaven with "the key of the abyss and a great chain in his hand" and will bind the Satanic dragon for 1000 years (Revelation: 20:1).

He assuredly remains the undisputed hero in the first war against Satan: in single combat he defeated the arch-fiend and hurled him down from heaven. Another, more popular version of this is of course the one in which he subdues the dragon-Satan, although now St. George has monopoly on these great serpents.

Michael is usually shown with an unsheathed sword which signifies his role as God's great champion. In a curious passage in Daniel, God speaks in an uncharacteristically humble fashion, admitting that He had been unavoidably delayed in keeping a promised appointment with the prophet. The reason He gives is that Cyrus, the Prince of Persia, had successfully resisted Him for twenty-one days. He tells Daniel "but Michael, one of the leading Princes, has come to my assistance." He confesses that "In all this there is no one to lend me support except Michael, your Prince, on whom I rely to give me support and re-inforce me." From this we can deduce that Michael was the guardian angel of Israel, but it also appears he is the only one who backed up the Throne when the chips were really down.

There are Muslim traditions which describe Michael in wondrous form. "Wings the colour of green emerald . . . covered with saffron hairs, each of them containing a million faces and mouths and as many tongues which, in a million dialects, implore the pardon of Allah." In the Koran it is said that from the tears shed by this great angel over the sins of the faithful, cherubim are formed.

In earlier Persian legends Michael is identified with Beshter, "the one who provides sustenance for mankind." In one Dead Sea Scroll, *The War of the Sons of*

Light Against the Sons of Darkness, Michael is named the "Prince of Light," who leads a host against the dark legions of Belial, Prince of Darkness. In this role Michael is Viceroy of Heaven which, oddly enough, was the title of the Prince of Darkness before he fell.

Michael is also known as the angel of the Last Judgement and, as the "weigher of souls," has a pedigree dating from when the tribes of Israel were in captivity in Egypt. There, the weigher of hearts of the deceased was Anubis. This Dog, or jackal-headed deity was identified with the most important star in the Egyptian sky, Sirius, the dog star. In Persia the star is known as Tistar, the "Chief," and the earlier Akkadian term was Kasista, which denotes a Prince or leader. Add a pinch of Hebrew (*sar* is commander or Prince) and we come very close to the "Prince and Commander of the Stars (angels) who is Michael." His peacock decorated wings recall the eye of the Egyptian Goddess, Maat, whose feather was weighed against a mortal's heart which lay in the balance of Anubis.

In the Middle Ages Michael was also held to be the "Psychopomp," the conductor of souls to the other world. As the Church was anxious to attract the old pagan worshipers of Roman Gaul, who remained faithful to the God Mercury, they endowed Michael with many of the attributes of that underworld God. Chapels dedicated to Michael sprang up over the ruins of the earlier temples which invariably had been built on hills or mounds. Thus Michael became, like Mercury, the guide for the dead. The many "Michael's Mounts" to be found throughout Europe and Britain attest to the power of that ancient archetype—the mound of the dead. Many of the sites were, in more ancient times, the focal points of Earth Forces known as Dragon Power so it is hardly a coincidence that Micha-el's fame should be connected with destroying the Dragon. Yet another curious link is to be found with the God-magician, Hermes, who in many cases is interchangeable with Mercury. The Greeks also called Hermes the Psychopomp, and his phallic spirit in the form of standing stones protected crossroads throughout the Greco-Roman world. While the Church banished all the earlier pagan deities to hell, in the case of Micha-el the various powers of all these Gods were absorbed within the Archangel's attributes.

It is foretold in Daniel that when the world is once again in real trouble Micha-el will reappear. Many scholars point to this century as being the one in which he will reveal himself once more in all his glory.

105

Malcolm

Godwin

ARCHANGEL GABRI-EL

The Sumerian root of the word Gabri is *GBR*, gubernator, or governor. Some argue that it means *Gibor*, power or hero. Gabri-el is the Governor of Eden and ruler of the Cherubim. But Gabri-el is unique amongst an otherwise male or androgynous host, for it is almost certain that this great Archangel is the only female in the higher echelons.

She is also the only angel mentioned in the Old Testament by name, except for Micha-el, and is said to sit on the left hand side of God, which is further evidence of her being female. To Mohammedans, Jibril/Gabriel dictated the entire Koran to Mohammed and is considered the angel of Truth (although devout Moslems will hardly agree to her female gender). Gabri-el is described as possessing 140 pairs of wings and in Judeo-Christian lore she is the Angel of the Annunciation, Resurrection, Mercy, Revelation and Death. As ruler of the first heaven, she is closest to Man. According to the testimony of Joan of Arc it was Gabri-el who persuaded the Maid of Orleans to help the Dauphin.

Gabri-el appears to Daniel in order to explain the prophet's awesome vision of the fight between the ram and the he-goat (the oracle of the Persians being overthrown by the Greeks). She appears again to Daniel to tell him of the coming of a messiah, a message which half a millenium later she repeats to Mary in the Annunciation. It is curious that she should appear at so many conceptions. Before Mary she had just announced to Zacharias the coming of John the Baptist.

The essentially female character of this remarkable Archangel is once again revealed in popular lore, which tells of how she takes the invariably protesting soul from paradise, and instructs it for the nine months while it remains in the womb of its mother.

Christien O'Brien, in *The Chosen Few* has put forward an interesting and closely argued case which supports Gabri-el's apparent interest in conception and birth. He suggests that she was once a real being in the biblical lands who experimented with the genes of early man and that Adam and Eve were amongst her first experiments. This real, down-to-earth being was then given supernatural powers by those inveterate deifiers, the Sumerians. There is a strange parallel with this hypothesis in the conflicting accounts of Matthew and Luke over the conception of Christ. In Matthew (1:20) the notably male Holy Ghost "begets Mary with

Malcolm

Godwin

child" while in Luke (1:26) it is Gabri-el who "came in unto her." As this can also be translated as "placing something within her" and as she then tells Mary that the conception is successful within her womb, it does raise a few questions if not a few eyebrows. Could such an otherwise primitive world have really had expertise in artificial insemination? Such an idea is much favored by those who believe that human beings are the outcome of experiments by extraterrestrials. But for the skeptics and those fundamentalists who remain unconvinced that female angels are possible, there is comfort in discovering that "Gabri-el" also can mean "Divine Husband."

St. Jerome tells us that when the archangel appeared to the Virgin she was mistaken for a man. Mary "was filled with terror and consternation and could not reply; for she had never been greeted by a man before." When she learned that it was an angel (or a female) she could converse freely for there was no longer anything for her to fear, or we might add, desire.

Like the great female angel Pistis-Sophia before her, Gabri-el once fell from grace for some unspecified misdemeanor. The angel Dobiel took her place for the period she was an outcast.

Archangel Rapha-el

"The Shining One who heals" was originally known as Labbi-el in Chaldea. The Hebrew term *rapha* meant "healer," "doctor" or "surgeon." As angel of healing he is often associated with the image of a serpent. He is known to be the chief ruling prince of the second heaven, chief of the Order of Virtues, guardian of the Tree of Life in Eden and by his own admission one of the seven angels of the Throne. This he reveals to Tobias in the book of Tobit.

In this account he travels with Tobit's son in disguise without letting on who he is until the journey's end. He shows Tobias, who has caught a huge fish, how to use each part of the creature, "the heart, the gall and the liver . . . these are necessary for useful medicines . . . and the gall is good for anointing the eyes, in which there is a white speck, and they shall be cured."

He is declared to be "one of the four presences set over all the diseases and all the wounds of the children of men" (Enoch 1), and in the Zohar is "charged to heal the earth . . . the earth which furnishes a place for man, whom he also heals of his illnesses."

He heals Abraham of the pain of circumcision since the patriarch had skillfully avoided this rite until old age, and cures Jacob of his disjointed thigh which he manages to get while wrestling with one of Rapha-el's colleagues.

Although officially a Virtue, he is said to have the six wings of a Seraph but at the same time belongs to the Cherubim, the Dominions and the Powers. He is said to be both the chummiest and funniest of all the angelic flock and is often depicted chatting merrily with some unsuspecting mortal. His sunny disposition is possibly due to his being Regent, or Angel of the Sun.

110

M a l c o l m

G o d w i n

Hebrews, 13.1–2

Let brotherly love continue.

Be not forgetful to entertain strangers: for thereby some have entertained angels unawares.

Leo Tolstoy

WHAT MEN LIVE BY

I

A shoemaker named Simon, who had neither house nor land of his own, lived with his wife and children in a peasant's hut and earned his living by his work. Work was cheap but bread was dear, and what he earned he spent for food. The man and his wife had but one sheep-skin coat between them for winter wear, and even that was worn to tatters, and this was the second year he had been wanting to buy sheep-skins for a new coat. Before winter Simon saved up a little money: a three-rúble note lay hidden in his wife's box, and five rúbles and twenty kopéks were owed him by customers in the village.

So one morning he prepared to go to the village to buy the sheep-skins. He put on over his shirt his wife's wadded nankeen jacket, and over that he put his own cloth coat. He took the three-rúble note in his pocket, cut himself a stick to serve as a staff, and started off after breakfast. "I'll collect the five rúbles that are due to me," thought he, "add the three I have got, and that will be enough to buy sheep-skins for the winter coat."

He came to the village and called at a peasant's hut, but the man was not at home. The peasant's wife promised that the money should be paid next week, but she would not pay it herself. Then Simon called on another peasant, but this one swore he had no money, and would only pay twenty kopéks which he owed for a pair of boots Simon had mended. Simon then tried to buy the sheep-skins on credit, but the dealer would not trust him.

"Bring your money," said he, "then you may have your pick of the skins. We know what debt-collecting is like."

So all the business the shoemaker did was to get the twenty kopéks for boots he had mended, and to take a pair of felt boots a peasant gave him to sole with leather.

Simon felt downhearted. He spent the twenty kopéks on vodka, and started homewards without having bought any skins. In the morning he had felt the frost; but now, after drinking the vodka, he felt warm even without a sheep-skin coat. He trudged along, striking his stick on the frozen earth with one hand, swinging the felt boots with the other, and talking to himself.

"I'm quite warm," said he, "though I have no sheep-skin coat. I've had a drop and it runs through all my veins. I need no sheep-skins. I go along and don't worry about anything. That's the sort of man I am! What do I care? I can live without sheep-skins. I don't need them. My wife will fret, to be sure. And, true enough, it *is* a shame; one works all day long and then does not get paid. Stop a bit! If you don't bring that money along, sure enough I'll skin you, blessed if I don't. How's that? He pays twenty kopéks at a time! What can I do with twenty kopéks? Drink it— that's all one can do! Hard up, he says he is! So he may be—but what about me? You have house, and cattle, and everything; I've only what I stand up in! You have corn of your own growing, I have to buy every grain. Do what I will, I must spend three rúbles every week for bread alone. I come home and find the bread all used up and I have to fork out another rúble and a half. So just you pay up what you owe, and no nonsense about it!"

By this time he had nearly reached the shrine at the bend of the road. Looking up, he saw something whitish behind the shrine. The daylight was fading, and the shoemaker peered at the thing without being able to make out what it was. "There was no white stone here before. Can it be an ox? It's not like an ox. It has a head like a man, but it's too white; and what could a man be doing there?"

He came closer, so that it was clearly visible. To his surprise it really was a man, alive or dead, sitting naked, leaning motionless against the shrine. Terror seized the shoemaker, and he thought, "Someone has killed him, stripped him, and left him here. If I meddle I shall surely get into trouble."

So the shoemaker went on. He passed in front of the shrine so that he could not see the man. When he had gone some way he looked back, and saw that the man was no longer leaning against the shrine, but was moving as if looking towards him. The shoemaker felt more frightened than before, and thought, "Shall I go back to him or shall I go on? If I go near him something dreadful may happen. Who knows who the fellow is? He has not come here for any good. If I go near him he may jump up and throttle me, and there will be no getting away. Or if not, he'd still be a burden on one's hands. What could I do with a naked man? I couldn't give him my last clothes. Heaven only help me to get away!"

So the shoemaker hurried on, leaving the shrine behind him—when suddenly his conscience smote him and he stopped in the road.

"What are you doing, Simon?" said he to himself. "The man may be dying of want, and you slip past afraid. Have you grown so rich as to be afraid of robbers? Ah, Simon, shame on you!" So he turned back and went up to the man.

II

Simon approached the stranger, looked at him, and saw that he was a young man, fit, with no bruises on his body, but evidently freezing and frightened, and he sat there leaning back without looking up at Simon, as if too faint to lift his eyes. Simon went close to him and then the man seemed to wake up. Turning his head, he opened his eyes and looked into Simon's face. That one look was enough to make Simon fond of the man. He threw the felt boots on the ground, undid his sash, laid it on the boots, and took off his cloth coat.

"It's not a time for talking," said he. "Come, put this coat on at once!" And Simon took the man by the elbows and helped him to rise. As he stood there, Simon saw that his body was clean and in good condition, his hands and feet shapely, and his face good and kind. He threw his coat over the man's shoulders, but the latter could not find the sleeves. Simon guided his arms into them, and drawing the coat well on, wrapped it closely about him, tying the sash round the man's waist.

Simon even took off his torn cap to put it on the man's head, but then his own head felt cold and he thought: "I'm quite bald, while he has long curly hair." So he put his cap on his own head again. "It will be better to give him something for his feet," thought he; and he made the man sit down and helped him to put on the felt boots, saying, "There, friend, now move about and warm yourself. Other matters can be settled later on. Can you walk?"

The man stood up and looked kindly at Simon, but could not say a word.

"Why don't you speak?" said Simon. "It's too cold to stay here, we must be getting home. There now, take my stick, and if you're feeling weak lean on that. Now step out!"

The man started walking and moved easily, not lagging behind. As they went along, Simon asked him, "And where do you belong to?"

"I'm not from these parts."

"I thought as much. I know the folks hereabouts. But how did you come to be there by the shrine?"

"I cannot tell."

"Has someone been ill-treating you?

"No one has ill-treated me. God has punished me."

"Of course God rules all. Still, you'll have to find food and shelter somewhere. Where do you want to go to?"

"It is all the same to me."

Simon was amazed. The man did not look like a rogue, and he spoke gently, but yet he gave no account of himself. Still Simon thought, "Who knows what may have happened?" And he said to the stranger: "Well then, come home with me and at least warm yourself awhile."

So Simon walked towards his home, and the stranger kept up with him, walking at his side. The wind had risen and Simon felt it cold under his shirt. He was getting over his tipsiness by now and began to feel the frost. He went along sniffling and wrapping his wife's coat round him, and he thought to himself: "There now—talk about sheep-skins! I went out for sheep-skins and come home without even a coat to my back, and what is more, I'm bringing a naked man along with me. Matrëna won't be pleased!"

III

Simon's wife had everything ready early that day. She had cut wood, brought water, fed the children, eaten her own meal, and now she sat thinking. She wondered when she ought to make bread: now or to-morrow? There was still a large piece left.

"If Simon has had some dinner in town," thought she, "and does not eat much for supper, the bread will last out another day."

She weighed the piece of bread in her hand again and again, and thought: "I won't make any more today. We have only enough flour left to bake one batch. We can manage to make this last out till Friday."

So Matrëna put away the bread, and sat down at the table to patch her husband's shirt. While she worked she thought how her husband was buying skins for a winter coat.

"If only the dealer does not cheat him. My good man is much too simple; he cheats nobody, but any child can take him in. Eight rúbles is a lot of money—he should get a good coat at that price. Not tanned skins, but still a proper winter coat. How difficult it was last winter to get on without a warm coat. I could neither get down to the river, nor go out anywhere. When he went out he put on all we had, and there was nothing left for me. He did not start very early today, but still it's time he was back. I only hope he has not gone on the spree!"

Hardly had Matrëna thought this than steps were heard on the threshold and some one entered. Matrëna stuck her needle into her work and went out into the passage. There she saw two men: Simon, and with him a man without a hat and wearing felt boots.

Matrëna noticed at once that her husband smelt of spirits. "There now, he has been drinking," thought she. And when she saw that he was coatless, had only her jacket on, brought no parcel, stood there silent, and seemed ashamed, her heart was ready to break with disappointment. "He has drunk the money," thought she, "and has been on the spree with some good-for-nothing fellow whom he has brought home with him."

Matrëna let them pass into the hut, followed them in, and saw that the stranger was a young, slight man, wearing her husband's coat. There was no shirt to be seen under it, and he had no hat. Having entered, he stood neither moving nor raising his eyes, and Matrëna thought: "He must be a bad man—he's afraid."

Matrëna frowned, and stood beside the stove looking to see what they would do.

Simon took off his cap and sat down on the bench as if things were all right.

"Come, Matrëna; if supper is ready, let us have some."

Matrëna muttered something to herself and did not move, but stayed where she was, by the stove. She looked first at the one and then at the other of them and only shook her head. Simon saw that his wife was annoyed, but tried to pass it off. Pretending not to notice anything, he took the stranger by the arm.

"Sit down, friend," said he, "and let us have some supper."

The stranger sat down on the bench.

"Haven't you cooked anything for us?" said Simon.

Matrëna's anger boiled over. "I've cooked, but not for you. It seems to me you have drunk your wits away. You went to buy a sheep-skin coat, but come home without so much as the coat you had on, and bring a naked vagabond home with you. I have no supper for drunkards like you."

"That's enough, Matrëna. Don't wag your tongue without reason! You had better ask what sort of man—"

"And you tell me what you've done with the money?"

Simon found the pocket of the jacket, drew out the three-rúble note, and unfolded it.

"Here is the money. Trífonov did not pay, but promises to pay soon."

Matrëna got still more angry; he had bought no sheep-skins, but had put his only coat on some naked fellow and had even brought him to their house.

She snatched up the note from the table, took it to put away in safety, and said: "I have no supper for you. We can't feed all the naked drunkards in the world."

"There now, Matrëna, hold your tongue a bit. First hear what a man has to say—!"

"Much wisdom I shall hear from a drunken fool. I was right in not wanting to marry you—a drunkard. The linen my mother gave me you drank; and now you've been to buy a coat—and have drunk it too! . . . Give me my jacket. It is the only one I have, and you must needs take it from me and wear it yourself. Give it here, you mangy dog, and may the devil take you."

Simon began to pull off the jacket, and turned a sleeve of it inside out; Matrëna seized the jacket and it burst its seams. She snatched it up, threw it over her head and went to the door. She meant to go out, but stopped undecided—she wanted to work off her anger, but she also wanted to learn what sort of a man the stranger was.

IV

Matrëna stopped and said: "If he were a good man he would not be naked. Why, he hasn't even a shirt on him. If he were all right, you would say where you came across the fellow."

"That's just what I am trying to tell you," said Simon. "As I came to the shrine I saw him sitting all naked and frozen. It isn't quite the weather to sit about naked! God sent me to him or he would have perished. What was I to do? How do we know what may have happened to him? So I took him, clothed him, and brought him along. Don't be so angry, Matrëna. It is a sin. Remember, we must all die one day."

Angry words rose to Matrëna's lips, but she looked at the stranger and was silent. He sat on the edge of the bench, motionless, his hands folded on his knees, his head drooping on his breast, his eyes closed, and his brows knit as if in pain. Matrëna was silent, and Simon said: "Matrëna, have you no love of God?"

Matrëna heard these words, and as she looked at the stranger, suddenly her heart softened towards him. She came back from the door, and going to the stove she got out the supper. Setting a cup on the table, she poured out some *kvas*. Then she brought out the last piece of bread and set out a knife and spoons.

"Eat, if you want to," said she. . . .

Simon cut the bread, crumbled it into the broth, and they began to eat. Matrëna sat at the corner of the table, resting her head on her hand and looking at the stranger.

And Matrëna was touched with pity for the stranger and began to feel fond of him. And at once the stranger's face lit up; his brows were no longer bent, he raised his eyes and smiled at Matrëna.

When they had finished supper, the woman cleared away the things and began questioning the stranger. "Where are you from?" said she.

"I am not from these parts."

"But how did you come to be on the road?"

"I may not tell."

"Did someone rob you?"

"God punished me."

"And you were lying there naked?"

"Yes, naked and freezing. Simon saw me and had pity on me. He took off his coat, put it on me, and brought me here. And you have fed me, given me drink, and shown pity on me. God will reward you!"

Matrëna rose, took from the window Simon's old shirt she had been patching, and gave it to the stranger. She also brought out a pair of trousers for him.

"There," said she, "I see you have no shirt. Put this on and lie down where you please, in the loft or on the stove."

The stranger took off the coat, put on the shirt, and lay down in the loft. Matrëna put out the candle, took the coat, and climbed to where her husband lay on the stove.

Matrëna drew the skirts of the coat over her and lay down but could not sleep; she could not get the stranger out of her mind.

When she remembered that he had eaten their last piece of bread and that there was none for tomorrow and thought of the shirt and trousers she had given away, she felt grieved; but when she remembered how he had smiled, her heart was glad.

Long did Matrëna lie awake, and she noticed that Simon was also awake—he drew the coat towards him.

"Simon!"

"Well?"

"You have had the last of the bread and I have not put any to rise. I don't know what we shall do tomorrow. Perhaps I can borrow some of neighbour Martha."

"If we're alive we shall find something to eat."

The woman lay still, and then said, "He seems a good man, but why does he not tell us who he is?"

"I suppose he has his reasons."

"Simon!"

"Well?"

"We give; but why does nobody give us anything?"

Simon did not know what to say; so he only said, "Let us stop talking," and turned over and went to sleep.

V

In the morning Simon awoke. The children were still asleep; his wife had gone to the neighbour's to borrow some bread. The stranger alone was sitting on the bench, dressed in the old shirt and trousers and looking upwards. His face was brighter than it had been the day before.

Simon said to him, "Well, friend; the belly wants bread and the naked body clothes. One has to work for a living. What work do you know?"

"I do not know any."

This surprised Simon, but he said, "Men who want to learn can learn anything."

"Men work and I will work also."

"What is your name?"

"Michael."

"Well, Michael, if you don't wish to talk about yourself, that is your own affair; but you'll have to earn a living for yourself. If you will work as I tell you, I will give you food and shelter."

"May God reward you! I will learn. Show me what to do."

Simon took yarn, put it round his thumb and began to twist it.

"It is easy enough—see!"

Michael watched him, put some yarn round his own thumb in the same way, caught the knack, and twisted the yarn also.

Then Simon showed him how to wax the thread. This also Michael mastered. Next Simon showed him how to twist the bristle in, and how to sew, and this, too, Michael learned at once.

Whatever Simon showed him he understood at once, and after three days he worked as if he had sewn boots all his life. He worked without stopping and ate little. When work was over he sat silently, looking upwards. He hardly went into the street, spoke only when necessary, and neither joked nor laughed. They never saw him smile, except that first evening when Matrëna gave them supper.

VI

Day by day and week by week the year went round. Michael lived and worked with Simon. His fame spread till people said that no one sewed boots so neatly and strongly as Simon's workman, Michael; from all the district round people came to Simon for their boots, and he began to be well off.

One winter day, as Simon and Michael sat working, a carriage on sledge-runners, with three horses and with bells, drove up to the hut. They looked out of the window; the carriage stopped at their door, a fine servant jumped down from the box and opened the door. A gentleman in a fur coat got out and walked up to Simon's hut. Up jumped Matrëna and opened the door wide. The gentleman stooped to enter the hut, and when he drew himself up again his head nearly reached the ceiling and he seemed quite to fill his end of the room.

Simon rose, bowed, and looked at the gentleman with astonishment. He had never seen anyone like him. Simon himself was lean, Michael was thin, and Matrëna was dry as a bone, but this man was like someone from another world: red-faced, burly, with a neck like a bull's, and looking altogether as if he were cast in iron.

The gentleman puffed, threw off his fur coat, sat down on the bench, and said, "Which of you is the master bootmaker?"

"I am, your Excellency," said Simon, coming forward.

Then the gentleman shouted to his lad, "Hey, Fédka, bring the leather!"

The servant ran in, bringing a parcel. The gentleman took the parcel and put it on the table.

"Untie it," said he. The lad untied it.

The gentleman pointed to the leather.

"Look here, shoemaker," said he, "do you see this leather?"

"Yes, your honour."

"But do you know what sort of leather it is?"

Simon felt the leather and said, "It is good leather."

"Good, indeed! Why, you fool, you never saw such leather before in your life. It's German, and cost twenty rúbles."

Simon was frightened, and said, "Where should I ever see leather like that?"

"Just so! Now, can you make it into boots for me?"

"Yes, your Excellency, I can."

Then the gentleman shouted at him: "You *can*, can you? Well, remember whom you are to make them for, and what the leather is. You must make me boots that will wear for a year, neither losing shape nor coming unsewn. If you can do it, take the leather and cut it up; but if you can't, say so. I warn you now, if your boots come unsewn or lose shape within a year I will have you put in prison. If they don't burst or lose shape for a year, I will pay you ten rúbles for your work."

Simon was frightened and did not know what to say. He glanced at Michael and, nudging him with his elbow, whispered: "Shall I take the work?"

Michael nodded his head as if to say, "Yes, take it."

Simon did as Michael advised and undertook to make boots that would not lose shape or split for a whole year.

Calling his servant, the gentleman told him to pull the boot off his left leg, which he stretched out.

"Take my measure!" said he.

Simon stitched a paper measure seventeen inches long, smoothed it out, knelt down, wiped his hands well on his apron so as not to soil the gentleman's sock, and began to measure. He measured the sole, and round the instep, and began to measure the calf of the leg, but the paper was too short. The calf of the leg was as thick as a beam.

"Mind you don't make it too tight in the leg."

Simon stitched on another strip of paper. The gentleman twitched his toes about in his sock looking round at those in the hut, and as he did so he noticed Michael.

"Whom have you there?" asked he.

"That is my workman. He will sew the boots."

"Mind," said the gentleman to Michael, "remember to make them so that they will last me a year."

Simon also looked at Michael, and saw that Michael was not looking at the gentleman, but was gazing into the corner behind the gentleman, as if he saw some one there. Michael looked and looked, and suddenly he smiled, and his face became brighter.

"What are you grinning at, you fool?" thundered the gentleman. "You had better look to it that the boots are ready in time."

"They shall be ready in good time," said Michael.

"Mind it is so," said the gentleman, and he put on his boots and his fur coat, wrapped the latter round him, and went to the door. But he forgot to stoop, and struck his head against the lintel.

He swore and rubbed his head. Then he took his seat in the carriage and drove away.

When he had gone, Simon said: "There's a figure of a man for you! You could not kill him with a mallet." . . .

VII

Then Simon said to Michael: "Well, we have taken the work, but we must see we don't get into trouble over it. The leather is dear, and the gentleman hot-tempered. We must make no mistakes. Come, your eye is truer and your hands have become nimbler than mine, so you take this measure and cut out the boots. I will finish off the sewing of the vamps."

Michael did as he was told. He took the leather, spread it out on the table, folded it in two, took a knife and began to cut out.

Matrëna came and watched him cutting, and was surprised to see how he was doing it. Matrëna was accustomed to seeing boots made, and she looked and saw that Michael was not cutting the leather for boots, but was cutting it round.

She wished to say something, but she thought to herself: "Perhaps I do not understand how gentlemen's boots should be made. I suppose Michael knows more about it—and I won't interfere."

When Michael had cut up the leather he took a thread and began to sew not with two ends, as boots are sewn, but with a single end, as for soft slippers.

Again Matrëna wondered, but again she did not interfere. Michael sewed on steadily till noon. Then Simon rose for dinner, looked around, and saw that Michael had made slippers out of the gentleman's leather. . . .

And he said to Michael, "What are you doing, friend? You have ruined me! You know the gentleman ordered high boots, but see what you have made!"

Hardly had he begun to rebuke Michael, when "rat-tat" went the iron ring that hung at the door. Someone was knocking. They looked out of the window; a man had come on horseback and was fastening his horse. They opened the door, and the servant who had been with the gentleman came in.

"Good day," said he.

"Good day," replied Simon. "What can we do for you?"

"My mistress has sent me about the boots."

"What about the boots?"

"Why, my master no longer needs them. He is dead."

"Is it possible?"

"He did not live to get home after leaving you, but died in the carriage. When we reached home and the servants came to help him alight, he rolled over like a sack. He was dead already, and so stiff that he could hardly be got out of the carriage. My mistress sent me here, saying: 'Tell the bootmaker that the gentleman who ordered boots of him and left the leather for them no longer needs the boots, but that he must quickly make soft slippers for the corpse. Wait till they are ready and bring them back with you.' That is why I have come."

Michael gathered up the remnants of the leather; rolled them up, took the soft slippers he had made, slapped them together, wiped them down with his apron, and handed them and the roll of leather to the servant, who took them and said: "Goodbye, masters, and good day to you!"

VIII

Another year passed, and another, and Michael was now living his sixth year with Simon. He lived as before. He went nowhere, only spoke when necessary, and had only smiled twice in all those years—once when Matrëna gave him food, and a second time when the gentleman was in their hut. Simon was more than pleased with his workman. He never now asked him where he came from, and only feared lest Michael should go away.

They were all at home one day. Matrëna was putting iron pots in the oven; the children were running along the benches and looking out of the window; Simon was sewing at one window and Michael was fastening on a heel at the other.

One of the boys ran along the bench to Michael, leant on his shoulder, and looked out of the window.

"Look, Uncle Michael! There is a lady with little girls! She seems to be coming here. And one of the girls is lame."

When the boy said that, Michael dropped his work, turned to the window, and looked out into the street.

Simon was surprised. Michael never used to look out into the street, but now he pressed against the window, staring at something. Simon also looked out and saw that a well-dressed woman was really coming to his hut, leading by the hand two little girls in fur coats and woollen shawls. The girls could hardly be told one from the other, except that one of them was crippled in her left leg and walked with a limp.

The woman stepped into the porch and entered the passage. Feeling about for the entrance she found the latch, which she lifted and opened the door. She let the two girls go in first, and followed them into the hut.

"Good day, good folk!"

"Pray come in," said Simon. "What can we do for you?". . .

"I want leather shoes made for these two little girls, for spring."

"We can do that. We never have made such small shoes, but we can make them; either welved or turnover shoes, linen-lined. My man, Michael, is a master at the work."

Simon glanced at Michael and saw that he had left his work and was sitting with his eyes fixed on the little girls. Simon was surprised. It was true the girls were pretty, with black eyes, plump, and rosy-cheeked, and they wore nice kerchiefs and fur coats, but still Simon could not understand why Michael should look at them like that—just as if he had known them before. He was puzzled, but went on talking with the woman and arranging the price. Having fixed it, he prepared the measure. The woman lifted the lame girl on to her lap and said: "Take two measures from this little girl. Make one shoe for the lame foot and three for the sound one. They both have the same-sized feet. They are twins."

Simon took the measure and, speaking of the lame girl, said: "How did it happen to her? She is such a pretty girl. Was she born so?"

"No, her mother crushed her leg."

Then Matrëna joined in. She wondered who this woman was and whose the children were, so she said: "Are not you their mother, then?"

"No, my good woman; I am neither their mother nor any relation to them. They were quite strangers to me, but I adopted them."

"They are not your children and yet you are so fond of them?"

"How can I help being fond of them? I fed them both at my own breasts. I had a child of my own, but God took him. I was not so fond of him as I now am of these."

"Then whose children are they?"

IX

The woman, having begun talking, told them the whole story.

"It is about six years since their parents died, both in one week: their father was buried on the Tuesday, and their mother died on the Friday. These orphans were born three days after their father's death, and their mother did not live another day. My husband and I were then living as peasants in the village. We were neighbours of theirs, our yard being next to theirs. Their father was a lonely man, a wood-cutter in the forest. When felling trees one day they let one fall on him. It fell across his body and crushed his bowels out. They hardly got him home before his soul went to God; and that same week his wife gave birth to twins—these little girls. She was poor and alone; she had no one, young or old, with her. Alone she gave them birth, and alone she met her death.

"The next morning I went to see her, but when I entered the hut, she, poor thing, was already stark and cold. In dying she had rolled on to this child and crushed her leg. The village folk came to the hut, washed the body, laid her out, made a coffin, and buried her. They were good folk. The babies were left alone. What was to he done with them? I was the only woman there who had a baby at the time. I was nursing my first-born—eight weeks old. So I took them for a time. The peasants came together, and thought and thought what to do with them; and at last they said to me: 'For the present, Mary, you had better keep the girls, and later on we will arrange what to do for them.' So I nursed the sound one at my breast, but at first I did not feed this crippled one. I did not suppose she would live. But then I thought to myself, why should the poor innocent suffer? I pitied her and began to feed her. And so I fed my own boy and these two—the three of them—at my own breast. I was young and strong and had good food, and God gave me so much milk that at times it even overflowed. I used sometimes to feed two at a time, while the third was waiting. When one had had enough I nursed the third. And God so ordered it that these grew up, while my own was buried before he was two years old. And I had no more children, though we prospered. Now my husband is work-ing for the corn merchant at the mill. The pay is good and we are well off. But I have no children of my own, and how lonely I should be without these little girls! How can I help loving them! They are the joy of my life!"

She pressed the lame little girl to her with one hand, while with the other she wiped the tears from her cheeks.

And Matrëna sighed, and said: "The proverb is true that says, 'One may live without father or mother, but one cannot live without God.'"

So they talked together, when suddenly the whole hut was lighted up as though by summer lightning from the corner where Michael sat. They all looked towards him and saw him sitting, his hands folded on his knees, gazing upwards and smiling.

X

The woman went away with the girls. Michael rose from the bench, put down his work, and took off his apron. Then, bowing low to Simon and his wife, he said: "Farewell, masters. God has forgiven me. I ask your forgiveness, too, for anything done amiss."

And they saw that a light shone from Michael. And Simon rose, bowed down to Michael, and said: "I see, Michael, that you are no common man, and I can neither keep you nor question you. Only tell me this: how is it that when I found you and brought you home, you were gloomy, and when my wife gave you food you smiled at her and became brighter? Then when the gentleman came to order the boots, you smiled again and became brighter still? And now, when this woman brought the little girls, you smiled a third time and have become as bright as day? Tell me, Michael, why does your face shine so, and why did you smile those three times?"

And Michael answered: "Light shines from me because I have been punished, but now God has pardoned me. And I smiled three times, because God sent me to learn three truths, and I have learnt them. One I learnt when your wife pitied me, and that is why I smiled the first time. The second I learnt when the rich man ordered the boots, and then I smiled again. And now, when I saw those little girls, I learnt the third and last truth, and I smiled the third time."

And Simon said, "Tell me, Michael, what did God punish you for? and what were the three truths? that I, too, may know them."

And Michael answered: "God punished me for disobeying Him. I was an angel in heaven and disobeyed God. God sent me to fetch a woman's soul. I flew to earth, and saw a sick woman lying alone who had just given birth to twin girls. They moved feebly at their mother's side but she could not lift them to her breast. When she saw me, she understood that God had sent me for her soul, and she wept and

130

Leo

Tolstoy

said: 'Angel of God! My husband has just been buried, killed by a falling tree. I have neither sister, nor aunt, nor mother: no one to care for my orphans. Do not take my soul! Let me nurse my babes, feed them, and set them on their feet before I die. Children cannot live without father or mother.' And I hearkened to her. I placed one child at her breast and gave the other into her arms, and returned to the Lord in heaven. I flew to the Lord, and said: 'I could not take the soul of the mother. Her husband was killed by a tree; the woman has twins and prays that her soul may not be taken. She says: "Let me nurse and feed my children, and set them on their feet. Children cannot live without father or mother." I have not taken her soul.' And God said: 'Go—take the mother's soul, and learn three truths: Learn *What dwells in man*, *What is not given to man*, and *What men live by*. When thou hast learnt these things, thou shalt return to heaven.' So I flew again to earth and took the mother's soul. The babes dropped from her breasts. Her body rolled over on the bed and crushed one babe, twisting its leg. I rose above the village, wishing to take her soul to God, but a wind seized me and my wings drooped and dropped off. Her soul rose alone to God, while I fell to earth by the roadside."

131

Leo

Tolstoy

XI

And Simon and Matrëna understood who it was that had lived with them, and whom they had clothed and fed. And they wept with awe and with joy. And the angel said: "I was alone in the field, naked. I had never known human needs, cold and hunger, till I became a man. I was famished, frozen, and did not know what to do. I saw, near the field I was in, a shrine built for God, and I went to it hoping to find shelter. But the shrine was locked and I could not enter. So I sat down behind the shrine to shelter myself at least from the wind. Evening drew on, I was hungry, frozen, and in pain. Suddenly I heard a man coming along the road. He carried a pair of boots and was talking to himself. For the first time since I became a man I saw the mortal face of a man, and his face seemed terrible to me and I turned from it. And I heard the man talking to himself of how to cover his body from the cold in winter, and how to feed wife and children. And I thought: 'I am perishing of cold and hunger and here is a man thinking only of how to clothe himself and his wife, and how to get bread for themselves. He cannot help me.' When the man saw me he frowned and became still more terrible, and passed me by on the other side. I despaired; but suddenly I heard him coming back. I looked up and did not recognize the same man: before, I had seen death in his face; but now he was alive and I recognized in him the presence of God. He came up to me, clothed me, took me with him, and brought me to his home. I entered the house; a woman came to meet us and began to speak. The woman was still more terrible than the man had been; the spirit of death came from her mouth; I could not breathe for the stench of death that spread around her. She wished to drive me out into the cold, and I knew that if she did so she would die. Suddenly her husband spoke to her of God, and the woman changed at once. And when she brought me food and looked at me, I glanced at her and saw that death no longer dwelt in her; she had become alive, and in her too I saw God.

"Then I remembered the first lesson God had set me: '*Learn what dwells in man*.' And I understood that in man dwells Love! I was glad that God had already begun to show me what He had promised, and I smiled for the first time. But I had not yet learnt all. I did not yet know *What is not given to man*, and *What men live by*.

"I lived with you and a year passed. A man came to order boots that should wear for a year without losing shape or cracking. I looked at him, and suddenly, behind his shoulder, I saw my comrade—the angel of death. None but me saw that angel; but I knew him, and knew that before the sun set he would take that rich man's soul. And I thought to myself, 'The man is making preparations for a year and does not know that he will die before evening.' And I remembered God's second saying, '*Learn what is not given to man.*'

"What dwells in man I already knew. Now I learnt what is not given him. It is not given to man to know his own needs. And I smiled for the second time. I was glad to have seen my comrade angel—glad also that God had revealed to me the second saying.

"But I still did not know all. I did not know *What men live by*. And I lived on, waiting till God should reveal to me the last lesson. In the sixth year came the girl-twins with the woman; and I recognized the girls and heard how they had been kept alive. Having heard the story, I thought, 'Their mother besought me for the children's sake, and I believed her when she said that children cannot live without father or mother; but a stranger has nursed them, and has brought them up.' And when the woman showed her love for the children that were not her own, and wept over them, I saw in her the living God, and understood *What men live by*. And I knew that God had revealed to me the last lesson, and had forgiven my sin. And then I smiled for the third time."

XII

And the angel's body was bared, and he was clothed in light so that the eye could not look on him; and his voice grew louder, as though it came not from him but from heaven above. And the angel said: "I have learnt that all men live not by care for themselves, but by love." . . .

And the angel sang praise to God, so that the hut trembled at his voice. The roof opened, and a column of fire rose from earth to heaven. Simon and his wife and children fell to the ground. Wings appeared upon the angel's shoulders and he rose into the heavens. And when Simon came to himself the hut stood as before, and there was no one in it but his own family.

Howard Schwartz

The Bridegroom

and the Angel of Death

(Yemen: 14th century)

There once was a righteous man named Reuben who had but one son, whom
he had begotten after his eightieth year. During Reuben's long life he had commit-
ted a sin but once. On that occasion he came into the synagogue and found another
man sitting in his place. He rebuked him, and the man immediately went away and
sat by the door weeping bitterly. When his tears reached the Throne of Glory, God
took pity on his plight. Therefore, he sent the Angel of Death to take Reuben's son,
who was about to be wed.

When the Angel of Death came into his house, Reuben recognized him at once
and said, "Why have you come here? Has the time come for me to accompany
you?" "No," replied the angel, "God has sent me to take your son's life." "Why?
He has not yet even stood beneath the marriage canopy and known his hour of
joy." "Because you rebuked the poor man who sat in your place," the angel replied.
And Reuben understood that his sin had counted greatly against him, and that the
punishment was much worse than if his own life were sought.

Reuben pleaded with the angel to give his son thirty days in which he might
marry and taste a little joy before his life was snatched away. And because of
Reuben's merits, the angel agreed to wait that long before he returned to take his
son's soul.

Now God was very angry with the Angel of Death for postponing the death of Reuben's son, and He rebuked the angel for disobeying. So the angel decided to revenge himself when the time came to take Reuben's son by taking him with the same fourfold anger that the Lord had shown against the angel. When twenty-nine days had passed, and one day remained before the wedding was to take place, the Prophet Elijah came to Reuben's door. The young man, who opened the door, trembled when he saw him and asked to know why he had come. Then Elijah said: "Know, my son, that tomorrow the Angel of Death will come to take your soul." The young man grieved greatly to learn this, since that was also to be the day of his wedding.

Then the young man pleaded with Elijah and asked if there was anything he could do to save himself. Elijah said, "When you are standing beneath the marriage canopy, you will notice a poor man dressed in dirty and torn clothes. Give honor to him, for that is how the Angel of Death will disguise himself, and perhaps he will have mercy upon you."

The next day, as the bridegroom stood with his bride beneath the wedding canopy, he saw the poor man that Elijah had described sitting beside the door. He went over to him and said: "Master, I wish to do you honor. Come, sit in the distinguished place before the Ark." To which the old man replied: "May He to whom honor is due have compassion upon you." He then went and sat under the canopy, with the young man before him. And the father of the young man, who knew that the Angel of Death was due to come that day, recognized him and prostrated himself before him and sobbed and pleaded for the life of his child, entreating the angel to take his life instead.

Then the Angel of Death clothed himself with his garments of cruelty, anger, wrath, and severity, unsheathed his sword, and put his foot upon the old man's neck, in order to slay him. At this the father's limbs trembled and shook, and he stood up and fled from the angel, saying, "Go ahead, take him for whom you have been sent, for I cannot bear thee." Now when the bridegroom's old mother saw this, she fell down and entreated the angel to spare her son and to take her life instead. And while she was sobbing and weeping, the Angel of Death again donned his garments of cruelty, so that he appeared like a warrior going forth to battle. He unsheathed his sword and placed his foot upon her neck to slay her, but she fled from him in terror and said: "Spare me. Take him for whom you have been sent. For I cannot bear to look upon you."

Now the bride, standing beneath the canopy, had witnessed all that had happened. She prostrated herself before the Angel of Death and said: "I entreat you to spare the life of my bridegroom and to take my life instead. And again the angel clothed himself in his terrible garments, so that all who saw him shrank away in terror. He drew his sword and placed his foot upon her neck. Yet she did not run away, as had the others, but said: "Finish the bidding of the King of Kings, who has sent you." And when the angel saw that she was not afraid to die for her groom, a tear of mercy fell upon her from his eye.

Then God, who had witnessed all that had taken place, said: "If this cruel one has mercy upon them, shall I, who am called the God of Mercy, not have compassion?" And God thereupon granted seventy more years to them both.

Howard

Schwartz

S i r d a r   A l i   I k b a l   S h a h

Spell for the Manufacture and Use of a Magic Carpet

Let a virgin girl weave a carpet of white and new wool, in the hour of the sun, when the moon is full, and when the sun is in Capricorn. Go into the country, to an uninhabited place, where you will suffer no disturbances; spread your carpet facing East and West, and, having made a circle to enclose it, hold your wand in the air, and call upon Michael toward the East, Raphael to the North, Gabriel to the West, and Miniel to the South. Then turn to the East and invoke the name of Agla. Take in your left hand the point of the carpet that is to the East, then turn toward the North and do the same; repeating it similarly for the South and the West, until you have raised all four corners. Then turning again toward the East, say, reverently:

Agla, Agla, Agla, Agla: O God Almighty, who art the life of the Universe, and who ruleth over the four divisions of its vast form by the strength and virtue of the four letters of Thy Holy Name: Tetragrammaton Yod He Vau He. Bless in Thy name this covering which I hold, as thou hast blessed the mantle of Elijah in the hands of Elisha; so that, being covered by Thy wings, nothing may be able, to injure me, even as it is said "He shall hide thee under his wings, and beneath His feathers shall thou trust."

Then, fold it up, saying Recabustira, Cabustira, Bustira, Tira, Ra, A; and keep it carefully until you next need it. Choose a night of full or new moon. Go to a place

where you will suffer no interruption, having written the following characters on a strip of azure blue virgin parchment with the feather of a dove:

RAZIEL

Then prostrate yourself, after casting some incense on the fire; holding the wand in your left hand, the parchment in your right, say:

Vegale, Hamicata, Umsa, Terata, Yeh, Dah, Ma, Baxasoxa, Un, Horah, Himesere O God, Thou Vast One, send unto me the inspiration of Thy light, and make me to discover the secret thing which I ask of Thee, whatsoever such and such a thing may be. Make me to search it out, by the aid of Thy Holy Ministers Raziel, Tzaphniel, Matmoniel, Io.

Iona and Peter Opie

Traditional Verses

Matthew, Mark, Luke, and John,

Matthew, Mark, Luke, and John,
Bless the bed that I lie on.
Four corners to my bed,
Four angels round my head;
One to watch and one to pray
And two to bear my soul away.

God bless this house from thatch to floor,
The twelve apostles guard the door.
Four angels to my bed;
Gabriel stands at the head,
John and Peter at my feet,
All to watch me while I sleep.

Acknowledgments

"A Tree Full of Angels" from *A Tree Full of Angels: Seeing the Holy in the Ordinary* by Macrina Wiederkehr. Copyright © 1988 by Macrina Wiederkehr. Reprinted by permission of HarperCollins Publishers, Inc.

"Spirits" by Robert Bridges, reprinted from *Poetical Works of Robert Bridges* (1936) by permission of Oxford University Press.

"A Very Old Man with Enormous Wings" from *Leaf Storm and Other Stories* by Gabriel García Márquez and translated by Gregory Rabassa. Copyright © 1971 by Gabriel García Márquez. Reprinted by permission of HarperCollins Publishers, Inc, Carmen Balcells and Jonathan Cape Publishers.

"The Possibility of Angels" from *The Possibility of Angels* by Keith Bosley. Copyright © 1969, Macmillan General Books.

"Jacob Wrestles with the Angel" from *Legends of the Jews* vol. 1, by Louis Ginzberg. Reprinted by permission of the Jewish Publication Society of America.

"Angel Surrounded by Paysans" from *Collected Poems* by Wallace Stevens, copyright © 1950 by Wallace Stevens. Reprinted by permission of Alfred A. Knopf Inc. and Faber and Faber Ltd.

"Archangel" from *Pigeon Feathers and Other Stories* by John Updike, copyright © 1962 by John Updike. Reprinted by permission of Alfred A. Knopf Inc. and Penguin Books Ltd.

"25th June, Diaries 1914" from *The Diaries of Franz Kafka* by Franz Kafka, edited by Max Brod and translated by Joseph Kresh and Martin Greenberg, copyright © 1938 Max Brod. Reprinted by permission of Schocken Books, Inc.

"Saints and their Angels" from *Know Your Angels: The Angel Almanac*, copyright © 1993 by John Ronner (Mamre Press).

"Angel Levine" from *The Magic Barrel* by Bernard Malamud. Copyright © 1958, and copyright renewed © 1986 by Bernard Malamud. Copyright © The estate of the late Bernard Malamud. Reprinted by permission of Farrar, Straus & Giroux, Inc.

"William Blake Talks About Angels" from *The Oxford Book of Literary Anecdotes* edited by James Sutherland (1975) & originally *The Cabinet Gallery of Pictures* by Allan Cunningham (1833). Reprinted by permission of Oxford University Press.

"The Angel" from *The Poetry and Prose of William Blake*, edited by David B. Erdman, reprinted by permission of Bantam Doubleday Dell Publishing Group, Inc.

"Angels, in the Early Morning" from *The Poems of Emily Dickinson*. Reprinted by permission of the publishers and the Trustees of Amherst College from *The Poems of Emily Dickinson*, Thomas H. Johnson, ed., Cambridge, Mass. The Belknap Press of Harvard University Press, Copyright © 1951, 1955, 1979, 1983 by the Fellows of Harvard College.

"The Angel of Conception" from *Gabriel's Palace: Jewish Mystical Tales* by Howard Schwartz.